GOSSAMER

LOIS LOWRY

HOUGHTON MIFFLIN COMPANY BOSTON 2006

Walter Lorraine  Books

FOR NADINE

We are such stuff
As dreams are made on;
* and our little life*
Is rounded with a sleep.

—William Shakespeare,
The Tempest, Act 4, Scene 1

Walter Lorraine (wℓ) Books

Copyright © 2006 by Lois Lowry
All rights reserved. For information about permission
to reproduce selections from this book, write to Permissions,
Houghton Mifflin Company, 215 Park Avenue South,
New York, New York 10003.

www.houghtonmifflinbooks.com

Library of Congress Cataloging-in-Publication Data
Lowry, Lois.
  Gossamer / by Lois Lowry.
      p. cm.
  "Walter Lorraine Books."
  Summary: While learning to bestow dreams, a young dream giver
tries to save an eight-year-old boy from the effects of both his abu-
sive past and the nightmares inflicted on him by the frightening
Sinisteeds.
  ISBN-13: 978-0-618-68550-9
  ISBN-10: 0-618-68550-2
  [1. Dreams—Fiction. 2. Nightmares—Fiction. 3. Foster home care—
Fiction.4. Child abuse—Fiction.]   I. Title.
  PZ7.L9673Gos 2006
  [Fic]—dc22   5\06   2005030849

Printed in the United States of America
QUM   10 9 8 7 6 5 4 3 2 1

GOSSAMER

1

An owl called, its shuddering hoots repeating mournfully in the distance. Somewhere nearby, heavy wings swooped and a young rabbit, captured by sharp talons, shrieked as he was lifted to his doom. Startled, a raccoon looked up with bright eyes from the place where he was foraging. Two deer moved in tandem through a meadow. A thin cloud slid across the moon.

❧

The pair crept stealthily through the small house. Night was their time of work, the time when human conversation had ceased, when thoughts had drifted away and even breathing and heartbeats had slowed. The outdoors was awake and stirring but the little house was dark and silent.

They tiptoed, and whispered. Unaware, the

woman and her dog slept soundly, though the dog, on his pillow bed of cedar shavings at the foot of the woman's four-poster, moved his legs now and then as if chasing a dream rabbit.

"Are we a kind of dog?" Littlest One asked suddenly.

"Shhh."

They crept through the bedroom, out into the dark hall.

"May I talk now?"

"Oh, all right. Very quietly, though."

"I asked if we are a kind of dog."

Littlest One, whose name was sometimes shortened affectionately to simply Littlest, was working on this night with Fastidious, the one who had been designated her teacher. Littlest was very small, new to the work, energetic and curious. Fastidious was tired, impatient, and had a headache. She sniffed in exasperation.

"Whatever makes you ask such a thing? The other learners never ask questions like that."

"That's because they don't take time to think about things. I'm a thinker. Right now I'm thinking about whether I am a kind of dog."

"You just tiptoed past one. What did you notice about him?"

Littlest One thought. "A slight snore, a whiff of

doggy breath, and his upper lip was folded under by mistake, just above a big tooth. It gave him an odd expression."

"Does he resemble us in the least?"

Littlest pondered. "No. But I believe there are many kinds of dogs. We saw that book, remember."

"Hurry along," Fastidious said. "There's much to do, and we have to go down the stairs yet."

Littlest One hurried along. The stairs were difficult, and she had to concentrate.

"You do remember the book, don't you? Ouch!" She had stumbled a bit.

"Grasp the carpet fibers. Look how I'm doing it."

"Couldn't we flutter down?"

"We can't waste our flutters. They use up energy."

They both made their way carefully down. "I hear there are houses that have no stairs," Fastidious murmured in an irritated tone. "None at all. I sometimes wish that I had not been assigned this particular house."

Littlest looked around when they reached the bottom of the stairs. She could see now into the large room with the very colorful rug. The small-paned windows were outlined in moonlight on the floor by the rug's edge. "I think this house is lovely," she said. "I wouldn't want any other house."

They tiptoed across. Littlest noticed her own shadow in the moonlight. "My goodness!" she exclaimed. "I didn't know we had shadows!"

"Of course we do. All creatures have shadows. They are a phenomenon created by light."

A *phenomenon created by light. What a fine phrase,* Littlest thought. She twirled suddenly on the rug and watched her shadow dance.

"Why is your shadow darker than mine?" she asked Fastidious, noticing the difference just then.

"I'm—well, I'm *thicker* than you. You're barely formed yet. You're practically transparent."

"Oh." Littlest examined her own self and saw that it was true. She had not paid much attention before to her own parts. Now she touched her ears, watching the shadow's arms move, too; then she swiveled her neck to peer down at her own tiny behind.

"I do not have a tail," she announced. "I think I am not a dog. *We,* I mean. We are not a kind of dog."

"There. You have answered your own question. Come more quickly, please. You are dawdling."

Reluctantly, Littlest scurried across the design of the carpet, beyond the moonlit rectangles, and onto the pine-boarded floor, which was always a little dangerous because of splinters.

"What if the dog woke? Would he see us? Or

smell us, perhaps? I know he has a very significant nose. And if he did see us, or smell us, would that be dangerous for us?

"Or the woman? She woke the other night, remember? Because there was a bat in the house? It swooped and woke her somehow. She didn't like the bat. She was quite brave, I remember, and opened a window so the bat flew out into the night, which was where he had wanted to be all along, doing his night food-finding.

"But what if our little footsteps and flutterings had woken her? Would she have seen us?

"Are we visible to her?

"I know we don't fly the way bats do, but we operate at night. Might we be a type of bat?"

Fastidious turned suddenly with a very annoyed gesture. "Enough! Hush! Stop that questioning! We have our work to do. You insisted on coming. You said you'd be quiet. My nerves are becoming frayed. I want no more questions now. None whatsoever."

"All right. I promise," Littlest One said obediently. They continued on, one following the other.

"Are you doing your assigned tasks?"

"Yes. I touched the rug. And I'm touching this sweater now, the one she left on the chair."

"Gently. Do not under any circumstances *press*. But linger and get the feel of it into yourself."

5

"Yes, I am. You showed me how." Littlest was running her tiny fingers carefully over the sweater's soft sleeve. Then she touched a button and let her hand linger on it. It was startling, what she felt during the lingering. The entire history of the button came to her, and all it had been part of: a breezy picnic on a hillside in summer long ago; a January night, more recently, by the fire; and even, once, the time that a cup of tea had been spilled on the sweater. It was all there, still.

They moved quietly around the room, touching things. Fastidious half fluttered, half climbed to a tabletop and methodically touched framed photographs. Littlest watched in the moonlight and saw how the fingers chose and touched and felt the faces gazing out from the photographs: a man in uniform; a baby, grinning; an elderly woman with a stern look.

Forgetting her promise of no questions, Littlest suddenly asked, "Might we be *human?*" But Fastidious did not reply.

2

The woman stirred slightly in her sleep. She was dreaming. Sometimes, in her dreams, she recalled earlier times when she had been happier. When that occurred, her eyelids fluttered and the corners of her lips moved slightly in an upward curve.

Sometimes the creaking walls of the old house disturbed her sleep, or a shutter that came loose in the wind startled her briefly awake. A few nights before, a bat had found its way into the room, making squeaking sounds as it swooped through the dark. Sometimes a mouse scampered across the floor, usually in the fall when outdoor creatures sought warmth. Occasionally she thought that she should get a cat. Women her age often kept cats as company.

But she had the dog. They were growing old together and were good friends to each other. The dog made her take walks and gave her someone to talk to. He was all she needed.

The dog and the house. And her dreams. The tiny footsteps that crossed her bedroom each night never woke her.

3

"She talks constantly. Asks questions. Is much too curious." Fastidious sniffed imperiously and listed her complaints.

"What sorts of questions does she ask?"

They were back inside their place now, the gathering place of the dream-givers, the place they called the Heap. Littlest, exhausted, had curled into her own special corner and was asleep. But the bigger ones were meeting. Most Ancient was concerned about Littlest One.

"Oh, the usual," Fastidious replied irritably to his question. "The same things we've all wondered about. Who we are. Whether we might be a kind of *dog*, for heaven's sake! She asked that tonight. I should never have let her see that book about dogs. But it was on the woman's coffee table. It needed touching, and she was with me."

Most Ancient smiled. "She's very sweet, actually. I

don't think we've ever had one quite so curious. It's appealing."

"And she *plays*."

"Plays?"

"Dances about. And—well, as an example, I'd been teaching her about the delicacy of touch? Next thing I knew, she was chanting something under her breath, and when I asked her what on *earth* she was mumbling about, she said she'd created a tongue twister out of my instructions!"

"A tongue twister? What was it?" Most Ancient looked amused.

"I'd prefer not to say," Fastidious said primly.

"Come on. Tell," he coaxed.

"Well, all right, then." She sniffed. "It was this: *Flutter, flicker, and trutter*—no. *Flutter, tricker*—no." Fastidious took a deep breath and spoke very slowly. "*Flutter, flicker, and trickle; flutter, flicker, and trickle*. Completely silly, if you ask me.

"It's a nuisance," she added. "We started her too soon."

Most Ancient, smiling, looked around at the others. They were all resting after the nightly tasks. The actual touching wasn't exhausting. It was the moving around, climbing things, fluttering—which was very difficult and energy-consuming—and remembering what to touch. Stairs were hard to navigate. It made one tired. And that didn't even take into account the most arduous and important part of the job: the *bestowal*. Most Ancient was a little concerned about how Littlest One would take to that. It was one thing to play and giggle during the touching. But bestowal was a serious and demanding task. Perhaps Fastidious was correct and Littlest wasn't up to it yet.

∾

"Others? Opinions, any of you?"

One of the others yawned. "She'll be fine. I think she's cute, actually. Just keep an eye on her. We were all curious like that, once. Maybe not quite as talkative."

Most Ancient smiled. "Yes, that's true. Most of us were. I know I was. Do you think you can bear with it a while longer, Fastidious, until she settles down a bit?"

Fastidious sighed. "I suppose so. But—"

"I could switch you with someone else. Is there anyone who'd be willing to trade places?" He looked around.

Thin Elderly raised his hand. "I'd rather have that

house, as a matter of fact. My assigned house is very spare, very minimalist. Not much to touch. It makes a dull night."

Most Ancient peered at him. "Have you ever supervised?"

"No. But I think I'd do a good job. I like little ones."

"And you?" Most Ancient turned to the one who had raised the problem. "How would you feel about switching?"

Fastidious shrugged. "I'd be happy to have a dull night. Does the other house have stairs?"

Thin Elderly said no. Modern house, no stairs.

"Let's do it, then. I have increasing trouble on the stairs."

"Done." Most Ancient made a note in his book. "Anything else?" He looked around. But most of them were asleep now. They lay sprawled in the Heap, cuddled against each other. One snored slightly. One was murmuring, *"Flutter, flitter—?"*

"Well then," he went on, and tucked the book away. He yawned. "Another night's work well done, all of you.

"Sweet dreams," he added with a chuckle. It was his favorite joke.

4

This gathering, this dwelling place where they slept now, heaped together, was only one, a relatively small one, of many. It was a small subcolony of dream-givers. Every human population has countless such colonies—invisible always—of these well-organized, attentive, and hard-working creatures who move silently through the nights at their task.

Their task is both simple and at the same time immensely difficult.

Through touching, they gather material: memories, colors, words once spoken, hints of scents and the tiniest fragments of forgotten sound. They collect pieces of the past, of long ago and of yesterday. They combine these things carefully, creating dreams. Then they insert the dreams as the humans (and sometimes animals, for occasionally they give dreams to pets, as well) sleep.

The act of dream insertion is called *bestowal*. It is

very delicate. It requires absolute precision to bestow a dream, or even to decide exactly when one should be bestowed.

Littlest, the one who was only learning, had not yet studied bestowal. She was beginning the way they all had, with the touching, the gathering of material.

And she was learning, too, to dissolve.

"Concentrate," Fastidious had told her. "Stay very still, focusing on your own form."

Littlest stayed motionless and tried to concentrate on her small wisp of a self.

I wish I had wings, she thought. *Everything would be easier if we had wings. I could swoop and glide, and I would never tumble on the staircase because I would simply—*

"You are not concentrating!" Fastidious's voice was exasperated.

"Sorry," Littlest said apologetically, opening her eyes. "I was just thinking—"

"That's the point! You are not supposed to think! Focus on your form and will it to break down and dissolve."

Dutifully Littlest tried again—carefully *not* thinking, not paying attention at all to the thoughts that tried to swim into her mind, the questions about dogs, or wings, or all the many things she wondered about—and when she did that, focusing only on her own small form, she felt it begin to happen for the first time. She felt the pieces of her, the very tiniest pieces (she did not know if they even had a name) begin to separate.

"I'm doing it!" she called out gleefully. "It's working!"

Then, of course, it ended. Littlest opened her eyes, knowing she had done it, at least a little bit, and hoping for praise from Fastidious.

But Fastidious had disappeared.

"Where are you?" Littlest called in alarm. Then she realized. "Oh, my goodness! You've dissolved!"

In front of her, particle by particle, Fastidious reappeared. She had a very annoyed look.

"Two things," Fastidious said. "One, do not *ever* call out when you are mid-dissolving. See what happened? The instant you cried, 'I'm doing it!'—"

"I stopped doing it," Littlest acknowledged, abashed.

"Two. Never, never, *never* call attention to the fact that someone else has dissolved! This was only a training session, of course, but if we had been *out there* . . ." Fastidious gestured toward the larger world, the human world. "Well! The reason for dissolving is to become—what?"

"Invisible," Littlest whispered.

"And we need to be invisible why?"

"So that humans won't see us. Or know about us."

"And if I am dissolved, out there, in the human world, and suddenly someone screams"—she glared at Littlest and imitated her voice with a shrill sarcasm—"'Oh, my goodness! You've dissolved!'"

"I'm sorry," Littlest said.

Fastidious sighed. She was tired and had a touch of headache. She didn't like children and was impatient with inexperience.

Perhaps it was a good thing that now Thin Elderly would take over the training of Littlest One.

5

Now morning came. The woman rose slowly. She was wide awake—she always woke early—but her joints were stiffened by sleep and she sat at the edge of the bed for a while, moving her ankles and knees, telling them to wake up and get going.

She had a sense of humor about herself.

"You make me feel like the Tin Woodsman in *The Wizard of Oz*," she said to her left knee. "Rusted and immobilized. I wish I could oil you."

She stood, after a moment, and stretched. Her nightgown was flowered flannel, the small bouquets of sweet peas on it faded from repeated washings. She slipped her bare feet into worn blue slippers.

"Good morning, Toby," she said, looking down at the dog, who yawned and thumped his tail. "What about some breakfast?"

Slowly Toby roused and stretched, his nose to the floor while his rump rose. He watched while she put on a robe and tied the belt. Then he followed her into the hall, down the stairs through the front parlor into the kitchen, and stood patiently beside the cupboard where his food was stored. He watched while she filled a kettle with water and set it on the gas burner. He watched while she found a teabag in the canister, took a thick brown mug from a cupboard, and dangled the teabag in it. He watched while she dropped a slice of bread into the toaster and turned the toaster on.

Finally she filled his bowl and set it on the floor beside the stove. Then, when the kettle whistled, she poured the steaming water into the mug.

"Another day," the woman said, as she took her plate of buttered toast and her cup of tea to the table. She unfolded a flowered cloth napkin and placed it in her lap after she had sat down. Toby, finished now with his gulped breakfast, curled by her feet in a spot where sun, finding its way through the small-paned window of the old house, had outlined a square on the floor.

"We'll take a walk after I get dressed," she told him. "How about that? It looks like a lovely morning."

Toby drummed the floor with his tail. They took a walk every morning unless the weather made it impossible. They always walked to the corner, turned left, walked past the Methodist church—many squirrels there, on that large lawn, but Toby no longer bothered about them—past the house of the young couple with the new baby, and across the street to the small park with the diagonal path where sometimes they stopped beside a fountain.

Resting on the park bench, the woman would listen to the birds and watch young parents push small children on the nearby swings as Toby sat attentively at her feet. Then they would continue on, around the next corner, and then the next, making a complete square and returning home. It was a short walk, but all that she could manage.

He dozed while she ate. She continued to talk to him though she knew he was asleep. She had no one else to talk to, no one but Toby. She had outlived many of her friends, as well as several earlier dogs.

Life had become very lonely for the woman, but she was accustomed to her solitude. She sipped her tea, sighed, and fingered a folded letter and its envelope that lay on the table. With a worried look she thought about the way her existence was about to change.

6

"Whatever became of Rotund? He used to curl near you in the daytime Heap." Littlest was chattering as she set out for the evening's work with her new supervisor. "I remember that you and Rotund used to tell jokes to each other. He always told one that started, 'A horse went into a bar.' What's a bar, by the way? I never understood that joke."

Thin Elderly shook his head and chuckled. He did like little ones, it was true, but he could see that this curious chatterbox was going to be a handful. "Shhh," he said. "Remember that we always move quietly."

"I am," Littlest whispered. "Look! Tiptoes!" She pointed to her own transparent, delicate feet. She skipped along beside Thin Elderly.

"I was just wondering about Rotund," she added. "I liked him. And I know he was a friend of yours."

Thin Elderly frowned. The thought of it was

painful to him. "He turned menacing," he told the little one. "We'll say no more about it. He is gone."

Turned menacing. Littlest did not know exactly what it meant, but she knew it was very, very bad. Those who turned menacing disappeared. Well, not disappeared. They still existed. But they were no longer part of the community of dream-givers. They had gone someplace else. Someplace frightening. Maybe even evil.

"Why do some of us turn menacing?" she whispered.

They were at the entrance to their assigned house, the little house with geranium-filled window boxes and the rocker on the porch, the place where the woman lived. In a minute they would enter, compressing themselves and sliding in through the space under the front door. Thin Elderly reached over and took Littlest's hand. The timing of her question was unfortunate, he thought, because they were about to start their night's work. But he was responsible now for her teaching.

"It just happens," he told her in a low voice. "We are not certain why. Some think it is because they have touched things too deeply. You must be aware of that. During the touching, be gentle. Do not *delve*."

"What is *delve*?" she whispered.

He tried to think of a way to explain the unexplainable. "You've learned touching, right?'

She nodded.

"You've been touching in here, correct?" He gestured toward the house they were about to enter. "Take your thumb out of your mouth."

Littlest removed her thumb reluctantly. "Yes," she said. "Lots. This house is filled with things."

"Good. My last house, the one I just traded to Fastidious, had so little. Flat empty tabletops. A lot of glass and steel. A crystal vase with a single flower? What an impersonal feel to it! It was very unreceptive to touching."

"You'll love this one," Littlest assured him.

"Give me an example of something you've been touching."

She concentrated on remembering her nights of gliding silently through the woman's house. "There are photographs," she said. "I like those. They're in frames, on tables in the parlor. And one beside her bed, but I haven't been allowed to touch there yet. Too dangerous."

Thin Elderly nodded. "Yes, you're a little noisy. Fastidious was wise not to let you too close yet."

"I'll have to be close, when I bestow," Littlest pointed out.

"Eventually. But you're still learning. Describe touching a photograph."

"Well, there's one I especially like. I'll show you when we're inside. It shows a man in a uniform, smiling. He has a very pleasant face."

"All right. And so you touch his picture—how?"

"Like this." Littlest raised one small hand and touched Thin Elderly very gently. She let her fingers flutter and linger, but the touch was barely perceptible.

Thin Elderly smiled. "Good!" he told her. "You have a gossamer touch."

Littlest looked at her own fingers and smiled proudly.

"Fastidious taught you well about touching. Tell me what happens when you touch the man's photograph."

Littlest thought. "I collect little—" She paused. "I can't remember what they're called."

"They can be called anything. I like to call them *fragments*," Thin Elderly told her.

She nodded. "I collect fragments. I store them inside myself. They make me feel good. There's a fragment of a party, and the man is laughing. There's a bit of dancing. And there's a—"

She paused, blushing, and giggled.

"Shhh," Thin Elderly reminded her.

Littlest One covered her mouth and stifled her own giggle. "There's a kiss," she said. "Well, a fragment of a kiss. I always like to collect that."

"All right," Thin Elderly told her. "It sounds as if you are quite good at touching and collecting. But here is what you must guard against. Always remember this." He leaned toward her and spoke very seriously.

"*Delving* means touching too deeply. Pressing your hand instead of using that lovely light flickering touch you just showed me. It sometimes happens unintentionally, when dream-givers become too interested in what they're touching. When they start to like it too much."

"Like the kiss?" Littlest whispered.

"Possibly. Never linger and press, because everything has a menacing underside. If you begin to pick up the menacing pieces . . ." He sighed.

"Even by mistake?" Littlest asked.

Thin Elderly nodded. "It's what happened to Rotund. He pressed and delved. Some of us could see it was happening. We tried to warn him, but—"

Littlest sighed. "Then he disappeared."

"Well, he had to go away. He became something else. You can't be a dream-giver when you become consumed by the dark side, the menace."

"What did he become, then?"

Thin Elderly shuddered. "Promise me you won't talk about this in the Heap."

"I won't. Cross my heart." Littlest touched her own pale wisp of a chest.

"The term is"—he lowered his voice and whispered the word—"*Sinisteed*. Don't ever say it aloud."

She looked puzzled. "*Steed* means 'horse,' doesn't it? I touched a picture of a beautiful horse in the woman's house."

"It's horselike," he acknowledged. "Four legs. Quite powerful. It stamps the earth, and the nostrils quiver. That's what Rotund is now. And others.

"But there is no beauty to it," he added. "It's hideous."

Littlest trembled a little. "Can it bestow?" she asked.

Thin Elderly gave a scornful laugh. "We bestow dreams," he reminded her. "But a . . ."—again his voice dropped to a whisper—"Sinisteed?" He pondered for a moment.

Then he said, "It *inflicts*."

"Inflicts?"

"Inflicts something called *nightmares*."

They remained silent for a moment. Littlest, glancing sideways to be certain he wasn't looking,

25

slid her thumb into her mouth again.

Finally he sighed. "Better get going. We have work to do. Mustn't delay. Fastidious told me about the woman. She needs a dream, and I haven't collected anything yet."

He looked down at Littlest. She withdrew her thumb.

"I have a lot of fragments," she told him, "but she never let me bestow."

"Well," Thin Elderly said, "time you learned, I guess. You say you have a party? And a kiss?"

Littlest nodded. "Fragments."

"We'll give her a very brief and gentle dream," he said. "I'll show you how."

Thin Elderly took her hand. "Come," he told her, and led her toward the door. Holding hands, they compressed themselves and slid in under. The night's work was beginning.

7

The woman shifted in her bed. Though it was late, she had been wakeful, troubled by the letter that had arrived in yesterday's morning mail. She had found it on the floor, just inside the mail slot, where it had been shoved through with an oil bill and a notice of a half-price sale on tuna at the local grocery store.

"Whatever is this?" she had said aloud, speaking as she usually did, to the dog. Toby had watched as she turned the envelope over and over in her hand. Then she had gone to the kitchen table, sat, and ripped it open.

Now the letter, folded and returned to its envelope, was on the table beside her bed. Littlest could see it there, in the moonlight.

"Should I touch that?" she asked Thin Elderly, whispering.

He had seen it, too. "No. It might be troubling."

The woman stirred, as if she had heard something.

"Dissolve!" Thin Elderly commanded in a whisper. Littlest obeyed, and concentrated on seeping her form into nothingness. It was very exhausting. But it worked. When the woman blinked herself awake in the moonlit bedroom, startled by a tiny sound, she saw nothing.

They could still see her. They watched as she looked around, sighed, plumped her pillow, and lay her head back down. She closed her eyes. After a moment her breath was even and slow. She was asleep again.

"Reintegrate," Thin Elderly whispered. "And stay very still."

Together they returned to their working selves, casting visible shadows in the moonlight. Littlest glanced with delight at hers, and moved her arms up and down, making a sort of marionette of herself. She was not accustomed to shadows yet.

Thin Elderly looked pointedly at her and she blushed and stopped playing.

"I'm going to bestow a dream on the dog," Thin Elderly whispered, "partly to keep him occupied, and partly to show you how. You've probably watched Fastidious do it, of course, but we all have different styles."

"She didn't like me to look," Littlest whispered in reply. "But I peeked."

"You seem the kind who would peek," Thin Elderly said, in an amused but slightly scolding tone. "What did you see, when you peeked?"

"She fluttered up and hovered. Then I think she breathed into the woman's ear. It was hard to see. She got very close. But I think she breathed."

Thin Elderly nodded. "It's the standard method. It's what she would have done. Fastidious is not very—"

He hesitated. "Well," he said, "I shouldn't criticize. But she is not very creative."

"I am very creative," Littlest whispered, and made a shadow picture of a duck with her small hand against the wall. "Sorry," she said. She stopped and folded her hands politely.

"Stay quiet and watch," Thin Elderly instructed. "First I center myself. Then I pull up the fragments I want to use, so that they are right there, ready. You know how to pull up fragments?"

"Yes. I practice, in the Heap."

"Good. Now, for a dog, like this one, it is almost always food. I will hover near his head. Then I'll pull up fragments regarding food and bestow them. Ears are the easiest way. But do you see the problem with the dog?" He pointed.

Littlest nodded. She giggled a little, very quietly. "Hanging-down ears," she said.

"Yes. Many dogs have those. I will bestow through his nose instead. Actually, the nose is a dog's best entry. Watch, now."

He fluttered over close to the dog and hovered there. She could tell that he was centering himself, making himself calm and receptive. Then he quivered slightly. She knew he was pulling up fragments now. She had felt her own self quiver when she practiced the pulling-up.

While she watched, he leaned forward so that he was almost touching the dog's dark, moist nose. For a brief moment she saw something like tiny sparks flicker from him. It reminded her of a time when she had been gathering touches near the fireplace, which had earlier been aglow, warming the woman as she read in a rocking chair nearby. The fire was out and the woman long asleep upstairs. But suddenly, as Littlest had hovered nearby, a dark log had shifted and a tiny flurry of sparks had burst into a brief constellation. Watching Thin Elderly bestow a dream, she remembered that bright moment.

Finished, he fluttered back to her side. They watched the dog. Toby's tongue quite suddenly emerged from his mouth and licked his own dark whiskered lips in satisfaction as he slept.

"He's dreaming now," Thin Elderly said, "of food."

"I saw it go from you to him," Littlest said. "Little sparkles, just for a second."

"Yes, it's visible for a second."

"Do the sparkles hurt? Or maybe tickle?"

Thin Elderly frowned. "Don't think about that. I suppose there is a moment's tickle. Ignore it."

"It's hard to ignore a tickle," Littlest said. "Sometimes in the Heap, if I'm near that plump one—what's his name? I forget his name—he likes to tickle me, and—"

Thin Elderly looked sternly at her. She hung her head in apology, for chattering.

"I'm going to let you try it now, on the woman," he said.

"Into her ear?" Littlest asked. "Hers don't hang down."

"Yes. Flutter up there. Center yourself. Pull up the fragments. You'll do the kiss, remember?"

She nodded. "But how do I—"

"It will just happen. You pull up the fragments and hold them there and hold them there until suddenly you can't contain them anymore, and then—"

"It's like *sneezing!*" Littlest realized in amazement.

"Shhh."

"Sorry," she whispered.

31

"You're right. Like sneezing. They'll just burst from you. Your job is aiming."

"I'm good at that. I flutter right to things. I hardly ever miss."

"Well, then. Here you go. Remember the sequence?"

"Flutter up. Hover. Gather. Then—"

"You forgot *center*," he reminded her.

"Sorry. I flutter up. I hover. I center. I gather. Then I aim. And I hold and hold and hold until I sneeze!"

"Say 'bestow.' 'Sneeze' is rather crude."

Littlest nodded. "Bestow," she whispered. "Here I go!"

Silently, following the sequence exactly, Littlest One bestowed a dream for the first time.

And there in the darkened bedroom, during a dream that by morning would be forgotten, the lonely woman became a girl and was kissed by a young soldier. At dawn she woke with a vague feeling of happiness.

8

"Toby," she said, as she sipped her tea and turned the letter over and over in her hands, "how will we deal with an angry boy?"

The dog, his head on his paws, simply blinked. His tail tapped the floor briefly.

"I could say no. I had told her I'd take a little girl. I could explain that I'm not up to having a boy."

Toby eyed a fly that had settled on the rung of a nearby chair. If it were closer, he would have made a try for it, just for the sport. But he didn't feel inclined to bother with this one.

"I thought a little girl would brighten the house a bit. I could knit sweaters and mittens for her. Read stories."

She glanced through the kitchen window into the small yard. "I thought a girl might love the flower garden. I could help her plant something easy. I'm not sure what would grow this late in the summer.

Nasturtiums, perhaps. They grow quickly, and the flowers are so bright-colored. A little girl would enjoy that.

"I could teach a girl to bake cookies, the way my mother taught me."

She raised and lowered her shoulders, easing the ache that sometimes troubled her there. She stirred her tea, which was cooling now.

"I know it wouldn't be easy. She'd come from a troubled background. They explained that. She might have some bad habits, and it would take a lot of patience."

She chuckled slightly. "Well, I needed a patient mother myself. I was a handful, Toby; would you believe it? Of course, that was a long time ago. Sixty-five years ago that I—what is the age again?" She looked at the letter another time. "He's eight. I was eight almost sixty-five years ago.

"But I remember it. I could handle an eight-year-old girl, even one who had bad habits. We'd make rules. Not harsh ones. Just some simple rules, about bedtime, and homework, and helping around the house.

"My mother did that. Of course, in those days there were punishments that we wouldn't use now. Sometimes a switching. More often, up to my room, no supper, no reading—

"I suppose these days it would be no TV. I wonder if a little girl would mind too much that we don't have a television, Toby. I suppose I could get a small one but we'd have some strict rules about watching.

"Of course, it would be only for a few weeks. A child can do without television for a few weeks. We'd read a lot, I expect."

The woman glanced down at the dog and smiled. He was sound asleep. "I'm talking to myself. Again."

She took her teacup to the sink and began to wash the few dishes that were there. "Bird feeder needs filling," she said, looking through the window to the place where it hung from a low branch of the gnarled apple tree.

"I could ask the boy to do something like that. It could be one of his chores."

Carefully she dried the cup and saucer and replaced them in the cupboard. She washed the spoon.

"I wonder why they describe him as angry. What does an eight-year-old have to be angry about?"

She folded the linen towel in half and hung it neatly over the handle of the oven door. "Time for our walk, Toby!" The dog lifted his head and then rose eagerly at the sound of the familiar word. He went and stood beside her, waiting for the leash, which she had taken from the hook where it hung.

"His name is John," she told the dog as she leaned down to fasten the leash to his collar. "He's an angry little boy named John, and we must be very patient with him. He'll be here Friday."

9

In the Heap, Littlest One, half asleep, heard one of the older dream-givers make his way to the place where Thin Elderly was dozing. She could hear them talking softly and perceived that the conversation was about her. "She'll be fine," Thin Elderly replied to a murmured question. "She's clever. It's just her curiosity that interferes. But curiosity's a good thing, actually."

It had been a fairly easy night. Most nights were easy, she found, now that she had gotten the hang of it. They went about, collecting fragments by touching; she was good at that and enjoyed it. And Thin Elderly, now that he was in charge instead of Fastidious, had found untouched places: the dishes, for example. Fastidious had never once touched dishes.

The woman's dishes, which had come to her from her own mother, were filled with important and meaningful fragments. Touching, Littlest could perceive all sorts of things: a child (the woman, probably, though it was hard to tell for certain) sulking, seated alone at a table after everyone else had gone. Refusing to eat something. Carrots, Littlest thought. It was a sweet memory, despite the sulking, because the child's mother, she perceived, had eventually taken the hated carrots away with a smile. With her gentlest touch, Littlest collected the child's petulant sulk, the woman's forgiving smile, a bib with an embroidered rabbit, and even the hand-painted flowers on a small blue plate. It would make a lovely dream, Littlest thought; she could combine it with the kitten she had collected from an old photograph, and perhaps some remembered music that she had found in the piano.

∾

In a somewhat distant place, in another Heap, a drowsy young dream-giver named Strapping was also thinking about dishes he had touched during his evening's mission. Strapping's territory, assigned as a kind of punishment, actually, because he had not been quite attentive enough to his duties, was an apartment on the first floor of a dilapidated house that stood unattractively in a yard thick with weeds and cluttered with discarded, forgotten things. It was not a good assignment, not a location that lent itself to happy dreaming, and he had groaned when he received it. But they told him that he would be promoted out of it after a while if he learned to work diligently and without complaint.

To his surprise, though, he had become oddly fond of the unkempt apartment and its unhappy occupant, a thin, sad woman who lived there alone and lit one cigarette from the end of the previous one. During his night visits he searched for pleasant fragments to touch and had found them, to his own surprise, in a folded sweater, a book left open, a broken seashell on a shelf, a badly framed snapshot of a small boy with a chipped front tooth. He brought those things to her, the memories they held, and gave them to her in dreams. Now and then she smiled in her sleep and he felt that he had done a tiny, invisible good deed.

Strapping had been surprised by the dishes, for he had been taught that dishes are thick with touchable fragments of happiness: pieces of birthday parties, holiday meals, families gathered at tables. But the woman's dishes, unmatched, stacked at random on an open shelf in her shabby, unclean kitchen, held only fragments of regret and sorrow. He found fear there, as well, for although the dishes he touched that night had been whole, they still contained fear fragments that involved smashing and breakage, tears and threats. No good dreams there. It was the stuff of nightmares, and he had finally turned away and left the kitchen, fluttering back to the small living area with its threadbare, filthy rug, the butt-cluttered ashtrays, and the outdated *TV Guide* on a table ringed with stains. An empty beer bottle stood on the table beside a half-eaten sandwich, but Strapping ignored those things.

He went once again to the painted shelf on the wall, to the seashell displayed there. It was the one object that he enjoyed the most, for touching it brought a breeze shot through with sunshine, the tangy whiff of salt, a child's laughter pealing across the breeze, and cool foam on bare feet sinking into their own outline in gritty sand at the ocean's edge. Collecting all of that at once was weighty. But Strapping was strong. He touched the shell, smoothing his touch around its perimeter, gathering the fragments to bestow the woman once again with the dream she loved and needed most.

This time, when he felt the shell, he felt too the sand-smudged hand of the child who had picked it up. He felt the warm lint-lined pocket of the boy's shorts as he placed the seashell there with others he had collected. Strapping gathered those things for the dream, so many things that he became heavy with them and had to move slowly to the room where the young woman slept.

As he leaned to breathe the dream into her, and felt the fragments—sand, sun, shell, foam, feet, pocket, salt, smile, all of them—begin their slide of transfer, the slide that would culminate in the barely perceptible burst of sparkles, he perceived, and added, the name of the boy. He was John.

Strapping fluttered back to watch her receive the dream. It was the part he enjoyed most, seeing the effect, the smile in the sleep, the happy sigh. It made him aware of how important his work was.

Tonight, upon receiving the dream, the young woman called out in her sleep, using the boy's name. "John!" she cried softly. She turned, her eyelids fluttering, and though Strapping could tell that she was basking in the dream and feeling the long-ago sun-filled day that he had brought back to her through the seashell, he sensed also that it had reminded her of a terrible loss.

10

He scowled when the woman called him Johnny. She held a paper in her hand, and he could see that his name was on it. His name was also printed in thick letters on a tag that flapped from the handle of his suitcase. JOHN. So why did the woman call him Johnny, a dumb nickname, a wimp name? He began to hate her for it. But he wouldn't let her know. He kept his face frozen, expressionless. He had mastered that. No one knew any of his feelings. He stared at the floor.

The social work lady was going over the paperwork with the woman. The woman would have to sign for him, as if he were a package from UPS—what a joke that was! The last people had signed for him too, and then returned him. Defective merchandise: you could always return that. Didn't fit. Wrong color. Missing parts.

Screw loose. Hah. Maybe that was his defect, the thing that got him sent back.

He had asked for Coke but the woman gave him lemonade. Holding the glass, he wandered into the next room, an ugly room with old-fashioned furniture and framed photographs of grouchy, old-fashioned people wearing stupid clothes. There was a man in a uniform, smiling, and the photo was tinted so the man's lips were pink, like a girl's. It wasn't even a good uniform like a Green Beret's or a Navy Seal's. John would be a Navy Seal if he could, someday. They swam carrying knives, then came to beaches at night and killed enemies there very silently before swimming away again. John wanted to do that.

There was a piano. Ruffled curtains, flowered wallpaper. He hated it all. And where was the television?

"Johnny!" It was the woman. He'd already forgotten her name, and didn't care. He wouldn't be here that long. He didn't need to call her anything. Especially if she kept calling him Johnny, not his name. He would call her Nothing. That would be her name. Hah.

He didn't reply.

He poked a key on the piano, a white one at

the far end, and heard the high sound it made.

"Johnny?" she said again, and now she was in the doorway, looking at him. "The lemonade stays in the kitchen. It's just a rule I have, so things don't get spilled on the furniture or the piano."

Rule I have. Rule I have. Fine. He had rules, too. One was don't smile back, even if they smile at you, and she was smiling at him now. She reached for the glass and took it from him.

"Do you like the piano? I took lessons on this very same piano when I was your age. My mother had to nag me to practice, but I'm glad she did."

He poked a key at the other end, and the sound was deep.

"If you like, I could teach you while you're here. I used to give lessons. I still have some old books around."

John shrugged and turned away.

"Have you met Toby?" she asked.

Oh, great. Someone else? One place he'd been had four kids besides him. One kept twisting his arm when no one was looking, then called him crybaby.

Toby was a crybaby name. He looked over then, thinking that, and saw that it was a dog. Not even a real breed, not a rottweiler or pit bull or anything. Just a mutt.

He reached out toward it without thinking, but it

backed away. It was scared of him. Good. He liked it when things were scared of him. It gave him power.

"Toby," the woman said to the dog, in a sweet, teasing voice, "be nice. Don't be scared. This is Johnny."

He glared at her. "*John,*" he said fiercely.

"Oh. I'm sorry. Here, John," she said to him, and reached into the pocket of her apron. She gave him a bone-shaped biscuit. "He's not used to boys. It's just been the two of us. But give him that and he'll be your new best friend." Then she turned and took the lemonade glass to the kitchen. The social work lady was at the door, holding her briefcase and preparing the fake goodbye smile she always used when she left him someplace new. He didn't look at her.

He looked at the dog. It stared back at him with big brown eyes. He had not been at a house with a dog before.

John knelt. "Here," he said, and held the biscuit toward Toby. Nervously, tentatively, the dog leaned forward. Its ears were upright, alert, its eyes on John's hand holding the treat.

A pink tongue appeared. Just as the dog was about to take the biscuit, John pulled it away. He laughed harshly, and Toby looked confused.

"Thought you'd get it, huh? Thought I liked you?" He spoke in a low voice so the woman wouldn't hear him. She was at the door, waving to the car the social work lady drove. It was a business car, with the city seal on its door. She probably didn't even have her own. She was probably married to some jerk who wouldn't let her have a car, who said she was a dumb broad, too dumb to drive. She had to take a bus to work, he figured.

Carefully he put the dog biscuit into his pocket. "I might give it to you later," he whispered to the dog. It was a good game, to get someone to believe you, even a dumb dog. Get them to trust you. Then surprise them. Hah. He'd keep pulling the biscuit away forever.

He pounded once with both hands on the piano. Then he went to the kitchen, picked up the glass from the table, and gulped the rest of the lemonade. If he didn't, she would take it away from him, hoping he would cry so she could hit him.

She was holding his suitcase now, and smiling at him. He frowned and wiped his sticky mouth with the back of one hand.

"Where's the TV?" he asked in a loud voice.

11

Sinisteeds rarely sleep. No sprawled snoozing Heap for them. They are a restless herd, these dark creatures who contain within them the most profound of all our fears, the hidden things, old guilts and failings that we will ourselves to forget. Their constant pawing and snorting is accompanied by an atmosphere of foul-smelling sweat, for they glisten with it. Their energy is boundless. They toss their heads and flare their nostrils, tasting the air, searching for the places where they will spew their loathsome holdings, waiting for deepest night, the time when infliction takes place.

They are not bound by rules or limits, as the dream-givers are. They prey on the most vulnerable. They have no mercy.

And they were aware of the boy. They were making ready for the boy.

Most Ancient called a meeting. The dream-givers gathered early in the evening, before dark fully fell, before they went out on their nightly work.

"A warning to you all," he announced. "I dislike bringing this up. It is not something we like discussing. But I'm feeling some early warning signs. Small tremors in the earth. I want you to be alert."

A murmur rippled through the Heap. Littlest One listened carefully. Around her, she heard the *sssss* sound. The dream-givers were saying the word under their breath.

Sinisteeds. Sinisteeds.

"They're convening," Most Ancient said. "I believe they have a victim identified. They've been on the prowl."

"Prowl?" Trooper asked. Trooper was a large, muscular dream-giver, forceful and decisive. "I'd say *rampage* is the word for it. I had to deal with one quite recently. It inflicted a terrible nightmare on a young man in my assigned house. Did a lot of damage. I've been doing remedial dreams ever since."

"I've had some trouble as well!" another voice called. Littlest peered toward the back of the Heap to see who was speaking. It was Dowager, so precise always, speaking now in a clipped tone. "I've been able to ward them off, but I've definitely felt some approaches. And I saw scorch marks on the wall of a bedroom."

"Scorch marks?" Littlest whispered in a questioning voice to Thin Elderly, who was beside her. "What are scorch marks?"

"I'll explain later," he whispered back.

"Anyone else?" Most Ancient looked around. Some heads nodded. A few hands went up.

"Well. We've always had these individual forays, of course. Trooper, good work. You do deal well with these. If any of you need help, feel free to call on Trooper for a little extra muscle.

"But what I want you all to be on the lookout for are signs of a pending group attack. I'm feeling a gathering starting. A Horde.

"This happens only rarely. Over the years, occasionally, they have focused on one victim, someone particularly helpless. Then they mass and descend. Perhaps only the oldest of you here have ever experienced it. Anyone remember the last Horde attack?" He looked around. "No one? Well, it's been a very long while.

"I don't mean to worry or alarm you. And I don't see it as *imminent*. But we must be on the lookout. Somewhere out there they are beginning to sniff—to sense—a victim. Let's be vigilant. Let's be on guard."

Subdued, the dream-givers rose from the Heap and began to set out for their night of work. There were apprehensive murmurs among them. Littlest could hear the whispered sound, *sssss*, that meant some of them were still saying the name under their breath.

"Sinist*eeee*d," she whispered to herself, testing the sound of it.

But Thin Elderly, looking down at her, shook his head in warning. He put his finger to his lips. Chastened and a little nervous, Littlest reached up, took his hand, and held tightly to it as they set out.

12

"I can't stay in a house with no TV," he said again. He was standing beside the piano with his hands clenched. The dog nosed at his sneakers but the boy didn't notice.

The woman knelt beside him, though she knew already not to reach out with a touch. Earlier she had tried to put her arm around him but he had flinched and pushed her away.

"You know," she said in a calm voice, "there are a lot of other things to do. I'll read to you, or you can read to yourself. There are plenty of books. Some left over from my own childhood. *The Bobbsey Twins*? I suppose that's more for girls. But there will be some book you'd like, I'm sure."

He rolled his eyes. "Get me a Game Boy, then, if

all you have are stupid books," he said.

"A what?" she asked, laughing. "I don't even know what that is. But if you like games, we can play games. Ever played Monopoly? I always lose, but I'm a pretty good sport. I have a Monopoly set in the cupboard over there, and Scrabble, and some others. I keep them for visiting children. I have a lot of grandnieces and grandnephews."

"I'm gonna run away," he announced. "Even if that door is locked I know how to open it. I'm out of here."

"Listen," the woman said, and tilted her head. "Hear that?"

They could both hear the sound of the heavy rain that had started to fall, and in the distance some rumbles of thunder.

"The door isn't locked. You can simply open it and walk through," she told him, "but it's nasty weather outside, and I'd be worried about you, about where you would sleep and what you'd find to eat.

"Why don't you wait until morning? At least this evening you'll have a nice dinner and a warm bed."

"I need TV."

"Well, I can't provide that, I'm afraid. But I do have a meatloaf in the oven."

He scowled. "Do you have ketchup?" he asked.

She nodded. "And ice cream for dessert."

"Do you have cards?"

"Cards?"

"You know, with A's and K's and Q's."

"Oh. Yes, I do, actually. Do you know some card games? We could do that after dinner."

"Okay," he told her, grudgingly. "I'll stay tonight. We can play war."

13

"Is it a Horde?" Littlest asked Thin Elderly in an apprehensive voice. She was trying hard to appear courageous and mature. The two were inside the house, huddled in the hallway between the bedrooms. The rain had stopped and there was a moon now; it illuminated the faded wallpaper, with its sentimental pattern of hoop-skirted ladies in gardens. It was dream-giving time, the darkest time of night, but the pair had not yet begun their work because of the sound of an approaching Sinisteed.

Thin Elderly was listening attentively. "No," he said. "It's alone."

Bravely, Littlest One made a tiny fist and held it up. "Shall I punch at it?"

"No. It's much stronger than we are. We can't fight it. We have to huddle here and watch it do its damage," Thin Elderly explained. "It'll probably choose only one: the woman or the boy. They don't much bother with dogs."

"What's that?" Littlest jumped, startled. "I can hear something right there by the window!"

"Hot breath. Exhalations," Thin Elderly whispered. "It's how they get in. They breathe themselves through the walls. That's the scorching you asked about."

The sound was increasingly terrible, first a snorting and heavy breathing, then a pawing against the wall of the house. Littlest thought she could even feel the heat of it and smell the acrid wet-smoke scent.

"Make yourself as small as possible," Thin Elderly instructed. "Don't bother dissolving. It won't bother us. It won't even notice us. It'll enter, probably through this wall right here, where we hear the breaths. Then it'll choose its victim, do the infliction—it's quite fast—and then gallop away. Try not to be frightened. But be small, to avoid being trampled."

"I don't want it to choose the boy," Littlest whispered in her tiniest voice. "He's not as strong as the woman. He cried in his bed before he slept."

Thin Elderly put his fingers gently over her mouth. "Shhh. Here it comes."

Together they withdrew into their very smallest selves and curled against each other silently while the beast entered, breathing itself an opening though the wall, searing the wallpaper, which peeled back with burned edges, and charring the plaster beneath. The noise became deafening—thumps and pounds and whinnies—but the woman and the boy continued to sleep. It was a sound that humans did not hear, and even the dog, with his heightened sense of hearing, perceived only a muffled thump and turned from one side to the other with a sigh.

Littlest, peeking, terrified, through her fingers, could see the eyes, bloodshot and angry, and smell its filthy, matted coat as it entered and stood, tossing its head. The beast filled the hallway, and its shadow against the wall in the moonlight was even larger. She trembled. But Thin Elderly was correct; it had no interest in her. It whipped its ropey mane back and forth with the tossing of its head, as if in decision-making, and then strode through the open door of the guest room and toward the bed where the little boy, in his striped pajamas, lay breathing evenly, one arm curled around a pillow.

The Sinisteed leaned its massive head down toward the boy and then, like an engine releasing steam, it snorted a hissing emanation of breath that enveloped the boy's head. *Sssssssssss!* It lasted only a second. Then the creature shook its head, whinnied triumphantly, and disappeared through the wall, which repaired itself instantly, into the night.

"Your first infliction," Thin Elderly told Littlest One. "Amazing, how quickly it happens, isn't it? You would have missed it if you had blinked."

He looked at her and she gave him a nervous smile.

"*Did* you blink?" he asked.

Littlest shook her head. "No," she said, "but I had my eyes closed tight. I was scared."

"Well," he told her, "there's really not much to see. The sound, though, is astonishing. That hiss. Now we must try to undo it."

"Undo it?"

"Have you gathered something calming to bestow on him?"

"Yes. But look!" Littlest said, pointing.

The boy had sat upright in the bed and was crying out. "Don't! Don't!" He turned his head from side to side, an odd repetition of what the beast had done. His eyes were closed but he continued to call out in panic. "Don't let him get me!"

"Drat!" whispered Thin Elderly. "It's too late. Stay here. Be quiet. Dissolve."

Littlest shrank herself into invisibility and Thin Elderly, beside her, did the same. Just in time. The woman, tying the belt of her robe, hurried from her own bedroom across the hall and into the room where the boy was calling.

"John!" she said in a firm, quiet voice. She sat on the bed and put her arms around him. He struggled, crying. "Help me!" he sobbed.

"Wake up, John," she said to him firmly. "You're having a nightmare."

In a moment his eyes opened and he looked around, whimpering. The bedroom was unchanged: his little suitcase was on the floor by the chair, his clothes draped over the chair's wooden arm. A nightlight glowed in the corner.

"Someone was—" the boy said. He blinked. "He was chasing me!"

"It was a nightmare," she told him again. "You're safe here."

He lay back down. She pulled the covers up over him and stroked his back through the blanket.

"I'll tell you a story," she said to him in a quiet voice.

"Okay."

"Once upon a time," the woman said, "there was a little boy. His name was John, and he was—"

"At the beach. He was at the beach with his mom," the boy said sleepily.

"Yes, he was at the beach with his mom on a

beautiful sunny day. It was warm, with a nice breeze. Seagulls were overhead, and—"

"Shells," he said, but his eyelids were fluttering and his voice was drowsy.

She glanced over to the table, where the boy had placed a delicate pink seashell that he had taken from his suitcase. "Yes," she said, "there were beautiful shells on the beach." She continued stroking him for a moment, whispering, "Shhh, shhh," until it was clear that he was sleeping again. She gazed at him briefly, then tiptoed back to her own bedroom.

From their watching place, Thin Elderly stirred himself and reemerged. Littlest did the same. "Now we have much work to do," he explained to her in a low voice. "Gather your best fragments. We must strengthen him."

14

"Who's this jerk?" John asked. He had taken a framed photograph from the piano and set it down on the kitchen table, where the woman was still sipping her morning tea.

She reached for it. "He was a friend of mine," she said, and touched the edge of the silver frame with her fingertips.

"Now he hates you, right? You *thought* he was your friend, right? But now he hates you."

"No, he never hated me. But this was a long time ago. We were both very young then."

"So where'd he go? California? I bet you don't even know. I bet he just left and didn't tell you where." John picked up his spoon and ate another mouthful of cereal, then made a face. "I hate this kind of cereal. I only like Sugar Pops."

"Don't eat it, then. I can make you some toast if you'd like." With her napkin she wiped the smudgy fingerprints from the glass that protected the old photograph.

The boy held a fingerful of soggy cereal under the table for Toby, then withdrew it quickly when the dog came to sniff. He wiped it on the knee of his jeans and kicked the dog lightly with his sneaker.

"I bet he never wrote to you or anything," he commented. "I bet he didn't send you any money. You should throw the dumb picture away."

"He wrote to me often. But then he died. Do you want toast?"

"Yeah."

She looked at him wryly. *"Yes, please?"* she said.

He repeated it sarcastically. She smiled, rose, and dropped two pieces of bread into the toaster on the counter.

"How did he die? Did he get murdered? I know somebody who got murdered."

"Not exactly. But he was shot."

The boy made his fingers into a gun. *"Blam,"* he said, and shot Toby, the dog. Then he shot the refrigerator. "I'm gonna get a gun," he said, and ate another spoonful of cereal.

"So did his wife shoot him or what?" he asked, with his mouth full.

"He didn't have a wife. He was killed in the war, in France."

"I know a poem about France: 'I see London, I see France—'" he began in a singsong voice, then interrupted himself. "Does your dog ever run away?"

"No. Toby always stays close to the house. He's always waiting for his next meal," she told him, laughing lightly.

"He'll die, though."

"Someday. But he's not terribly old. He'll probably live another, oh, maybe seven years. Won't you, Toby?" she said to the dog, who lifted his head at the sound of his name. She leaned toward him and scratched his neck.

"Well, if you don't want him anymore, you can get someone to shoot him. I'll do it for you after I get my gun."

"I'll never not want Toby," the woman told the boy. "There's your toast, popped up. I'll get some jam from the cupboard."

"Don't you ever get mad at him?" The boy lifted the two pieces of toast from the toaster and dropped them onto the blue plate on the table.

"Of course I do. Once he stood on his hind legs and grabbed a whole roasted chicken from the counter. I was furious."

"Did you beat him? I bet you beat him."

"No. But I called him a few not-very-nice names.

And I shut him in the back hall for a while."

"Did he cry?"

She laughed. "He whined. Piteously."

"Sometime you'll get really, really mad at him," John said. He tore one piece of toast in half and stacked the two pieces on top of each other. "Then you won't want him. You'll probably give him away.

"You'll probably give him to some jerk with no TV," he added matter-of-factly, and poked a hole through the remaining slice of toast with his index finger. "Can we play war again after breakfast?"

15

"I'm looking for a job," the young woman said into the phone. "But I've been busy. I moved, you know that. It was a pain in the neck to move.

"But I'm looking for a job now. I'm really cleaning up my act."

She exhaled some smoke and glanced with a wry look around the room, at the stacked unopened cartons, the stained rug, the dirty dishes, and an opened pizza box with the stale crusts still inside. "Not my *apartment*," she added under her breath.

"I know," she replied to a question from the person on the other end of the line. "Yes, I'm very aware that I have to be here for him. He'd be in school all day, and then I'd be home when he got home. I'm looking for something part-time, maybe like eight to two. I saw an ad for a receptionist and it said 'flexible hours.' I'm just about to call there."

She listened for a moment. She stubbed out her

cigarette and reached for the half-empty pack nearby.

"No, I wouldn't leave him alone again. Of course not." Nervously she twisted a strand of her long hair around one finger.

"And also," she went on, "I did what you suggested. I took out a restraining order."

She lit a cigarette and listened. "He's gone. I don't know where he is. I probably didn't even need the restraining order. I think he went to California.

"So anyway, as I said, I'm really getting it together. I'm going to counseling. But I need John back. It's totally weird having him gone. He's my best friend, you know?"

She listened and made a face, grimacing to herself. "No, well, I didn't mean that. I *know* he's my child. I know all that. I'll set limits. I can do all that stuff. But I need him back here so I can do it, right? I mean, how can I do *parenting* if my kid isn't here, right?"

She twisted her hair again, listening. Her shoulders, which had been tensely raised, sank, and her voice trembled slightly. "I lost it, okay? It was a bad time for me. I did some stupid things."

The voice on the telephone was calm, reassuring. The woman listened, rolling her eyes.

"Okay," she said in a defeated tone. "Okay. Yeah.

I understand. I know, it takes time.

"Listen, I'll call you back as soon as I get a job. And you make sure he's treated okay! And tell him—well, tell him I'm working on it, and he'll be back home soon, and I love him, and—"

Huddled on the couch, clutching the phone, the young woman began to cry. "Tell him I dreamed about him last night," she said.

16

"Do they come back to the same person again?" Littlest asked Thin Elderly. They were back at the Heap now, and most of the dream-givers were sleeping soundly, exhausted by their hard work during the night. But Littlest One was still thinking about the Sinisteed she had seen. Her thumb slipped into her mouth.

Thin Elderly put his arm around her. "They tend to, often," he said. "They make return visits and inflict what they call 'recurrences.'

"They won't ever hurt you," he reassured Littlest. "You needn't worry about that. But you will probably see that one again. I think he'll be coming back to the boy. We just have to hope that the Horde won't come with him. The boy is very vulnerable.

"They sense that," he explained. "They can sense when someone is weak, or in need."

The thumb popped out. "But the boy needs *me!*" Littlest said.

"Sorry," she added. "I meant, he needs *us.*"

Thin Elderly laughed affectionately. "Yes, he does," he told her.

"But I think he really needs me most," she confided, yawning, "because he's very little, for a human boy. And I know what it's like to be little."

"Well," said Thin Elderly, "it will serve him well, your understanding."

"We'll have to give him very good dreams."

"Yes, he needs every good dream we can bestow. We'll work very hard on strengthening the boy. I think we can even neglect the woman for a few nights. She's quite strong."

"But old," Littlest pointed out sleepily. "Very wrinkly and old." She glanced up at Thin Elderly and blushed. "Oops. Sorry."

"It's all right. I'm old, too, and wrinkly. I know that. And she is the same, that's true. And old people do need their dreams as much as anyone. But right now I feel we must concentrate on that little boy. He has so few fragments to hold on to, and some were destroyed during the infliction last night."

"The woman will help him, too. Remember when she told him a story and it helped him go to sleep?

'I'll tell you a story,' she said to him. I liked that."

"Yes. She's good with him."

"What's a story, exactly?" Littlest asked suddenly.

Thin Elderly looked at her with amusement. She had so very much to learn. "Let me think how to explain that," he said. "A story is—

"Well, *everything* is a story. Tell me something you've touched, in the woman's house."

"A button on her sweater."

"And what came from the button?"

"You mean the fragments?"

"Yes, the fragments. What were they?"

Thinking, Littlest scratched her nose. "There were lots. There was the time when Toby—that's the dog's name—"

"Yes," said Thin Elderly. "I know Toby."

"Well, he chewed the button once. He was just bored and there it was, something to do, so he chewed it. She scolded him, but she was laughing. That fragment's there."

"What else?"

"She spilled her tea, and it stained the button a little. And also—"

"Yes?"

"She was sad once, when she was wearing the sweater, and while she was feeling sad, she rubbed the button a little, back and forth. It comforted her.

It's a good fragment, because of the comfort.

"And one other time? This is funny! She held her niece's baby on her lap, and the baby grabbed the button and wouldn't let go! Everybody was laughing!"

"And all of that is there for you to find when you touch the button," Thin Elderly pointed out.

"And lots more."

"That is the button's *story*. All the things that have been part of the life of that little button. They create a story. Everything has a story," Thin Elderly explained.

Littlest thought it over. "And when she said to the boy, 'I'll tell you a story,' and then she began, 'Once upon a time there was a little boy,' that was *his* story, wasn't it?"

"Yes. Part of his story. A very small part."

"Then he went to sleep again. That was nice. I was afraid he wouldn't." She fell silent for a moment. "You know what, Thin Elderly?"

"What?"

"I'm scared that it will come back and it will bring the whole—I forget the name."

"Horde."

"Yes. I'm afraid of the Horde."

"We'll strengthen him. We'll fight the Horde by strengthening him. That's our job."

70

"It's an important job," she said sleepily. "But scary."

"It is indeed." Thin Elderly stretched and settled himself into a comfortable position. "Curl up now and get a good day's sleep," he said. "Tonight we'll start the strengthening. We'll have some hard work to do." He glanced over at Littlest One and smiled. Her wide eyes had already closed.

He closed his as well, and now the whole Heap slept and was silent, refreshing their vigor and strength for the work of the next night.

17

"Don't get any stupid idea about keeping me," John said. "Just because I did that stuff for you, filling the dog's dish and sweeping the porch, don't think you can keep me and make me be your slave."

They stopped briefly on the path through the park, to let Toby sniff a bush and raise his leg.

"I appreciated that," the woman told him, "the sweeping. It's hard for me because my shoulders are stiff. It was lovely to have help."

"C'mon, dog." John tugged at the leash and Toby moved to his side obediently. "The police would come if you tried to kidnap me," he pointed out. "They'd have sharpshooters, with rifles. They'd be behind every tree, aiming at your house. A guy would say into a microphone, 'Let the boy go.'"

"Goodness. That would cause some excitement in our quiet little neighborhood, wouldn't it?" She pointed to a wooden bench. "Shall we sit down for a moment? I get a little tired."

She arranged herself on the park bench and Toby settled himself at her feet. John sat beside her, kicking his feet restlessly. "Anyway, you couldn't keep me because I already have a mom and a dad. They're coming to get me. Maybe this afternoon."

He curled his hand into a spyglass and looked through it toward a squirrel at the foot of a nearby tree. "My dad has a shotgun," he said. "He could kill that squirrel. He could blow its head off.

"He could blow *your* head off!" he added, and turned toward her, still looking through his own curled hand.

"Goodness. Why ever would he do that?"

"Well, maybe he wouldn't. But if he found out you were mean to me, or something. Then he'd come all the way from California with his gun.

"I'd call him," he added. "I know how. He told me, 'You just call me if you need me. Anytime.' That's what he said."

"So you know your father's number in California?"

The little boy shrugged. "I don't need to. I just call that guy on TV. The Verizon guy."

"Oh. I see."

"It would cost a whole lot. And you'd have to pay. If you don't pay your phone bill, they keep calling to remind you, and if you still don't pay? Then they turn your phone off. Then how are you supposed to get a job or anything?"

The woman chuckled. She gathered her purse and sweater and stood. "Come, Toby, time to go home," she said. "Actually," she said to the boy as he wound Toby's leash around his hand, "I don't think I'll be looking for a job. I had one, once. I was a teacher. But I've been retired for quite a while.

"Is your mother looking for a job?" she asked, as they walked toward the park entrance. "Is that why you're worried about the phone?"

He scowled. "My mom don't need a job," he said. "She's rich. She lives in a mansion. She has bodyguards.

"Right now she's on vacation," he added. "That's why I have to stay with you and be your slave."

At the street corner, she put her hand lightly on his shoulder. "Wait for the walk light," she reminded him.

He held tightly to the dog's leash. "If it wasn't for me," he announced loudly, "this here dog would be roadkill."

The woman glanced down at Toby, waiting

patiently for the light to change. "You're probably right, John," she said.

"He's just a mutt, though." The walk light flickered on and they crossed the street. "Not worth anything. What did you pay for him? You probably got robbed."

The woman laughed. She looked down again at the scruffy mongrel, with his mottled fur and ragged ears. "Actually, I didn't pay anything for him," she explained. "I found him on my porch, freezing, one winter morning. He was just a puppy that someone had mistreated and then abandoned. But he's worth a lot to me, John. He's my closest friend."

They approached the little house and the woman took out her key to the back door. "Here we are, Toby. In you go." Opening the door, she unhooked his leash and the dog dashed inside to check his bowl.

The little boy followed, his untied sneaker laces flapping on the hall floor. "I might kidnap him," he announced. "You'd have to pay a thousand dollars to get him back, or else I'd kill him and mail you his ears."

"You hear that, Toby? You're in danger!" the woman said, looking down at the dog, who was lying on the kitchen floor beside his bowl. He looked up with his moist brown eyes, then yawned. His tail thumped once on the wooden floor.

"Why don't you give him a biscuit, John? He behaved so nicely on our walk. I like to give him a little reward from time to time." She pointed to the ceramic container with a molded bulldog on its lid. "They're in that jar."

The little boy took out a bone-shaped biscuit, felt its shape with his fingers, considered briefly, and then gave it to the dog, who accepted it with an eager gulp.

"Don't get used to this," John said to Toby, "because I'm out of here tomorrow."

18

"I have an idea," Littlest suggested to Thin Elderly. They were huddled together in the hallway again. It was the third night that the Sinisteed had roared through the wall and with his hissing breath inflicted a cruel nightmare on the little boy. For three nights they had watched helplessly during the infliction and then with concern as the woman had come in the night to comfort the boy when he cried out.

"And what would that be?" he asked her.

"I think I must touch the dog," she whispered solemnly.

Thin Elderly looked startled. "Surely you know that we do not touch living creatures," he said to her.

"Only for fear of waking them," she pointed out. "But the dog sleeps so very soundly. He even snores. And remember how light my touch is? Even when

Fastidious was mad at me, she still said I had a wonderful touch." She reached out and fluttered her fingers very lightly against him. "And you told me once that my touch was like gossamer.

"I don't know what that means, exactly," she added with a giggle.

"Gossamer is something very fragile and delicate," Thin Elderly explained. "Sometimes it means a cobweb."

"Oh. How sweet. I do love cobwebs. There was one in a corner of the woman's parlor once, behind the piano, and I danced in it. There was a moon that night, and it just seemed the thing to do, dancing in a moonbeam and a cobweb. Fastidious scolded me, though."

Thin Elderly smiled.

"My dancing touch was so delicate that I didn't even break the strands of the cobweb. I am quite, quite certain I could touch the dog."

Thin Elderly nodded. "Your touch is exquisitely dainty, Littlest One. I don't believe I've ever known a daintier one. And perhaps you would be able to touch the dog without waking him. But what good would it do?"

Littlest explained carefully, in a whisper. "The boy is so weak! And the nightmares come again and again."

Thin Elderly nodded sadly. "That's true," he agreed. "Each time they destroy more and more of the memories and fragments he has: the ones we've given him and the ones he brought with him."

"And he has so little for me to touch and give back to him in dreams, Thin Elderly. He has a chrysalis now, that he found out in the garden, and the woman let him keep it in a jar in his room. He's very gentle with it because she explained how a butterfly was being made inside. So it's a nice thing for me to touch—I can give him that fragment of gentleness and taking-care-of. But it's a very small thing. And there aren't many others.

"There's the pink seashell that he keeps on the table. And it's the most valuable thing, I think, because it has so many memories—I can feel them there—and it's part of his own story. Remember he wanted shells when she told him that story that began 'Once upon a time there was a little boy'?"

He nodded.

"But it's also very small," she sighed.

Thin Elderly smiled at her as she spoke so earnestly. She was barely larger than the seashell herself.

"There's a photograph, too, that he keeps in an inside pocket of his suitcase," she went on. "It's of a woman. There are a lot of fragments coming from that picture, but they're mixed. The feelings of them are all mixed up. I try to sift through and collect the good parts.

"And that's really all. His clothes don't give me much of anything. The social work lady bought his clothes. So really all I have—all that's worth touching—are the chrysalis and the seashell and the picture.

"But, Thin Elderly?" She looked up at him. "Guess what?"

He looked at her quizzically. "What?"

"He's starting to love the dog! I can *feel* it!"

"And so . . ." Thin Elderly, hesitating, considered what she had said.

"I need to touch the dog. Lightly, of course. In a very gossamer way. And I can give the boy that: the love feelings. Along with the gentle chrysalis feelings, and the warm happiness seashell feelings, and the good part of the photograph feelings.

"It will make it work better, adding in the dog! I'm sure of it. Make him much, much stronger against the nightmares."

She looked up at Thin Elderly. "Could I try, at least?" she pleaded.

Thin Elderly eased himself up from the huddling place. Three nights in a row they had had to hide this way, hunched over. He was achy.

"Come with me," he whispered. "The woman is

worn out from getting up at night. I'm going to bestow a wonderful, restorative dream on her. I've collected it from the parlor; I found it there in the old crocheted afghan she keeps over the back of the sofa. Her mother wrapped her in that afghan one Christmas morning when she was a very little girl. There was snow outside, and a new doll under the tree, and it was one of the happiest mornings of her life. I was quite delighted to find it there unused, ready to be collected.

"While I'm doing that, Littlest One, you may touch the dog."

"Oh, thank you, thank you," she whispered.

"No need for thanks," he replied. "No time. We must work quickly. We must try to help the boy."

19

"You say you allowed her to touch a dog?"

"I did, Most Ancient. The dog was sleeping deeply. And her touch is exquisite: very, very delicate. She calls it *gossamer*." Thin Elderly smiled.

Most Ancient, though he tried to look stern, smiled as well. "She's a dear little thing, isn't she? I cannot understand why Fastidious found her so difficult."

"Well," Thin Elderly replied, "she's Fastidious."

Most Ancient chuckled. "Still," he said, "we must keep in mind that the rules do prohibit touching living creatures. It's for our own safety, really."

"I understand. This did seem a special case, though."

They were seated together some distance from the Heap. Most Ancient no longer went out on the night work. He stayed here, pondering difficulties, adjudicating disputes, thinking deeply about the dream-givers and their responsibilities and problems. Thin Elderly had come to him at the end of the night, and while the others, including Littlest One, were arranging themselves for sleep, he had confided to Most Ancient the problem of the small boy, John, and confessed what he had done.

"The boy was weakening, you say." Most Ancient furrowed his brow, thinking about it.

"Yes. It was quite clear. He had suffered recurrent inflictions night after night. And Littlest had so few fragments to give him for strength. It was she who realized that he was beginning to love the dog."

"I've always been partial to dogs myself. Don't know why we don't have any. You'd think a dream-giving dog would be a great asset, wouldn't you? Could bestow on other dogs. I always found those ears difficult when I was bestowing. I remember once . . ."

Thin Elderly sighed. Most Ancient's mind wandered a bit these days. He tended to digress, to tell stories from the past, and sometimes the same stories again and again. Thin Elderly had heard this one several times. But he waited patiently until Most Ancient concluded.

Then he said, "I believe, sir, if you don't mind our going back to the problem of Littlest One, that she actually did the boy a great good. After she did the touching of the dog—and the dog didn't stir at all; he slept right through it—she immediately went across the hall, gathered herself and the new fragments, and fluttered up and bestowed them on the boy."

"Was there a reaction?"

"Immediately, sir. He had been restless, tossing, whimpering, and occasionally we heard him cry out in his sleep. The woman had hurried in to comfort him. She's had to do that night after night, and it's taking a toll on *her,* too. She's quite tired."

"So, let me see if I'm following this correctly. The boy had a nightmare—" Most Ancient sighed. "How I hate that word! But he had a nightmare, and cried out, and the woman comforted him. Where were you and Littlest then?"

"Huddled. Lately we've had to huddle a great deal. We have a special place in the hall, deep in the shadows by the attic stairs. Sometimes we dissolve."

"So the boy went back to his restless sleep. Do I have that right?"

"Yes. Tossing and turning."

"And the woman went back to her bed and to sleep. The dog?"

"Never woke. He sleeps right through every night."

"You waited, the two of you?"

"Yes. To give the woman time to get back to sleep. I was eager, actually, because I had a particularly wonderful dream to give her. I discovered some fragments in an afghan—"

"You're digressing," Most Ancient said, in a kindly way.

"Sorry. You're right." Thin Elderly chuckled, wondering if he was becoming as bad as Most Ancient. Old age did that to you.

"When did she touch the dog? Did you know she was going to? Did she have your permission?"

"Yes, she had asked permission and I had thought it over carefully and told her that she could. I knew it was against the rules. But this seemed a special situation. So we waited until the woman was asleep again, and the dog, of course, had never stirred at all. Then I went to bestow on the woman, and Littlest fluttered over and touched the dog. I finished my bestowal quickly. You probably remember, Most Ancient, how smoothly those good bestowals go, how quickly?"

Most Ancient nodded. "Yes. Very pleasurable."

"So I was able to watch while she touched the dog. It was truly exquisite, Most Ancient. She was smiling. You know how tiny she is. And still close to transparent, though she's starting to fill out. She fluttered here and there above the dog, reaching down; she seemed to concentrate on the neck area—"

"Why there, I wonder?"

"She explained later. It's where the boy most often strokes and scratches the dog. So there were many fragments there of affection and companionship. Those were the fragments she wanted."

"She has a keen sense for it, doesn't she?"

Thin Elderly nodded. "She does indeed. And to think: touching a living creature! I'd never seen it done before! She went about it as if it came naturally to her, and her touch was so—"

"*Gossamer.*"

Thin Elderly smiled. "Exactly."

"I believe we'll not make a fuss about the rule. It seems clear that she broke it for good reason, and of course with permission from you.

"The bestowal went well? Calmed the boy?"

"Oh, yes, immediately. She gave him a dream of the dog and he actually smiled in his sleep."

"Well, then," Most Ancient said, "we'll sleep now, too, Thin Elderly, you and I. It's been a long night's work, and we're both getting old." He added his usual little joke. "Sweet dreams."

20

The young woman glanced at the clock on the wall of the school office. Ten more minutes till she could take a break. Then she'd have to walk all the way out to her car and sit there to have a cigarette.

Last job she had, they could smoke out behind the kitchen. The waitresses all gathered there on breaks. Schools were different, though. She knew that. Of course they wouldn't want young kids seeing people indulging in bad habits. She hated that she'd smoked so much in front of John. Not as bad as what Duane did, though, she thought. Getting drunk all the time. Right in front of his own kid.

She sighed and looked back at the computer screen. It was pretty easy, the work. Good thing she'd taken that course. Duane hadn't wanted her to. He said she got good money in tips at the restaurant; what was she trying to do, turn into some kind of businesswoman or something? She was too dumb for that. Airhead, he called her.

But she had hung in there, had taken the course mornings, had traded her breakfast shifts with one of the other waitresses. Hadn't missed a class. And once she got the hang of it, the computer stuff was easy. It was all organized and made sense. There was a satisfying feeling to it, the way everything had a place and she could find it by clicking a few keys. It was mysterious to her, though, how it worked, how all of that information—there were three hundred kids in the school, and all of their files stored here—could be pulled forward by the touch of her fingers.

If only *life* were that easy!

"How's it going? You've been here, what? A week? Any problems?" A cheerful voice interrupted her daydreaming.

"It's going good. I'm getting the hang of it." The assistant principal, with his bright patterned necktie, was beside her desk, looking down at her with a smile. She'd forgotten his name. Walking through the office, he had stopped to see how she was doing. Nice of him. They were all nice here. She wouldn't tell him about the problem finding a place to smoke. For sure! He wouldn't have much sympathy for that.

"When school starts next week, it'll be a little crazy for a while," he told her with a chuckle. "A little noisy."

"Yes, sir. I won't mind."

"I wanted to thank you," he said.

"Thank me?" She looked at him nervously. Would he thank her for coming in this week, but now, after school starts Monday, they wouldn't need her anymore? Her heart sank. She *needed* this job. The hours were just right. John could be here, and she would see him during the day and know he was okay.

But no, he wasn't giving her notice. "The woman who called about enrolling her little girl?" he was saying. "I can't think of her name."

"It was Mrs. Merryman. And her little girl is Caroline."

"That's it. She told me you did such a good job with the school records from wherever it was—"

"Michigan," she reminded him.

"Yes. Thank you for that. That poor woman was so upset when she thought the records had been lost."

She laughed. It had been easy, solving that problem. And had felt good, soothing the distraught woman.

"Well." He turned to leave. Someone from the

front counter handed him a paper to sign. "Glad to have you with us."

"Thank you," she said shyly, and looked back at her computer. Soon, she thought, her son's name would be in there. The building would be noisy with children, and he could be one of them. "Hey, John!" she'd hear, in the hall, a kid calling to her boy, and the two would laugh at some joke, and there would be kids' artwork hanging on the walls, and one picture would have his signature: JOHN. She'd be so proud, then.

She just needed to *get him back*. That was the important, the urgent, thing. And she was making a start now. The apartment was cleaned up, sort of. She had a job. The assistant principal liked her, she could tell. And other people did. The principal's secretary had brought her a cup of coffee. The custodian said, "Good morning, Sunshine," to her every morning. One of the library assistants had asked where she got her shoes.

She could make friends, maybe. Duane had never let her have friends. The last time she'd had friends, she realized, was high school. After that it was just Duane, who wouldn't let her do anything but work, who wouldn't even let her drive.

And then, of course, there had been John. Her little boy, with his chipped tooth and curly hair.

Now they were both gone. Duane? Good riddance.

But she'd get John back. *Soon.*

She looked up at the clock again and decided to forget going to her car for a cigarette. Instead, she'd use her break to call the social worker.

21

"I think it helped. At least a little," Littlest whispered to Thin Elderly. "Look how he's smiling."

Together they watched the little boy's face. It did seem calmer, more rested than it had been. He lay on his side, snuggled against the pillow, with one arm curled around a shabby stuffed creature.

"Good work, Littlest One. And to think, you accomplished that with fragments from the dog!" Thin Elderly looked at her with admiration.

Littlest shook her head. "Not just the dog," she admitted. "I combined so many things that I almost ran out of breath! It was fragments from the seashell. And the chrysalis. And it was that other thing, too. See what he's holding?"

Thin Elderly leaned forward to examine the faded animal in the boy's arms. "I can't tell exactly what that is," he murmured.

"It's a very silly thing," Littlest explained. "A

kind of donkey thing, and very old—that's why its color is gone. One ear is mended, and it's patched on its behind. It belonged to the woman once. She called it—" Littlest giggled. "She called it Hee-Haw.

"She was just a little girl," she added, "but she saved it all these years. And she brought it down from the attic for the boy the other night, because he was having such trouble sleeping."

"How do you know all this?" Thin Elderly asked. "She would have done that during the day. You couldn't have been here then. We dream-givers come only when they're asleep.

"Come out to the hallway," he added. "We can converse more freely there."

They both looked again, fondly, at the sleeping boy, and then Littlest followed Thin Elderly to the corner of the hallway, the place where they had frequently huddled together during the invasions of the Sinisteed. Tonight the atmosphere was quiet, with nothing to fear. They would still be on guard, of course, but the visits of the hot-breathed intruder had become less frequent.

So the pair did not huddle apprehensively but rather settled comfortably in the shadowy hall corner beside the attic stairs.

"Now," Thin Elderly said, "tell me how you know so much. I'm in charge of you, Littlest One, and if you are doing anything dangerous, like stealing away from the Heap in daytime—"

"Oh, no! I wouldn't do that!" she reassured him.

"Daytime is a very, very hazardous time for us, you know. We are night creatures." His voice was solemn.

"What *exactly* are we, Thin Elderly?" Littlest One asked him. "I asked Fastidious again and again, but she never explained. At first I thought I might be a kind of dog, because I felt a kind of . . . well, I don't know how to describe it, but a kind of *brotherhood* with the dog—"

She giggled. "Or a sisterhood. But then I didn't have the right ears, and of course no *tail!*"

She wiggled her tiny bottom mischievously, and Thin Elderly smiled.

Then he became serious. "Littlest, stop changing the subject. I believe you that you have not ventured out in daylight. You're a very obedient little dream-giver, as a rule. But you must tell me how you are getting information. How did you know, for example, that the woman went to the attic in order to bring back that—"

Wrinkling his nose, he gestured toward the bedroom they had just left. "That *donkey* thing," he said.

"Hee-Haw," she reminded him with a grin.

"Yes. Hee-Haw." He said the name with a sound of amused disdain.

"Well," she said, "when I touch things—"

"Like the dog?"

"Like the dog, yes. But other things, too. The photographs, the seashell, the dishes, all of it, everything, even Hee-Haw—"

"Yes, even Hee-Haw." Thin Elderly smiled at the solemn look on the face of the tiny creature sitting by his side.

"It all seems to go together somehow," she explained. "The parts. The fragments. All the things that I collect—" She moved her fingers ever so lightly across his arm, to demonstrate.

"With your gossamer touch," he said.

"Yes. With my very gossamer touch I find them all together, waiting for a dream, and sometimes things are added in, things I didn't even know about, or touch. Like—well, like Hee-Haw."

She looked up at him. "He was part of the woman's childhood," she said. "Part of her story. 'Once there was a little girl, and she had a toy donkey—' would be the way her story begins. I already knew her story, from the things I'd collected. It's a long story, and it has sad parts. I get a lot of sad fragments from the photograph of the soldier—feelings of *never-coming-back*, feelings of *now-I'm-all-*

alone. But the kiss is there, too, in that photograph, so I always collect there, just to keep that kiss fragment for her.

"And you know what, Thin Elderly? Sad parts are important. If I ever get to train a new young dreamgiver, that's one of the things I'll teach: that you must include the sad parts, because they are part of the story, and they have to be part of the dreams."

"You'll be a good teacher one day," he told her.

"Thank you," she said demurely.

"But you must stop sucking your thumb."

She sighed. "I know. Soon I will."

❧

"Anyway," she said, changing the subject, "I felt as if I knew Hee-Haw a little, somehow, before she brought him from the attic. Then there he was! In the boy's room! And you know what, Thin Elderly?"

"What?" He smiled at her earnestness.

"I think maybe we gave her some fragments in a dream, some bits of her childhood, happy things, and there was Hee-Haw! She'd forgotten him until the dream! But then she remembered, and she went up to an old trunk, and found him again, and brought him to the boy.

"And somehow, when I saw him there, I understood about the trunk, and how the donkey had waited all those years to be given to a boy."

"And now the boy sleeps."

"We all helped him. You and I, and the woman, and the dog, and the donkey," Littlest pointed out, with a happy sigh. "We strengthened him." She giggled. "*Strengthen* is a hard word to say," she confided sleepily.

"Still," Thin Elderly reminded her, "we must be very watchful."

"Will—" She hesitated, not wanting to say the terrible name. "Will the S-things try to come back?"

"Oh, yes. I'm afraid so. They're always out there. I just hope—" He paused, not wanting to worry her.

"Hope what?"

"Oh, it's nothing."

"Please tell me. I'm brave. And I hardly ever do that with my thumb anymore, really."

"Well," he admitted, "Most Ancient still feels the Horde gathering. I'm fearful that they're frustrated by the boy's resistance.

"I'm afraid there is a Horde attack coming."

She looked at him, wide-eyed. He helped her to her feet and took her hand. "But not tonight, Littlest One," he said. "Tonight the boy is safe."

22

The young woman's dream-giver, Strapping, had had several different assignments in the past; he had bestowed many dreams. But his work had always, until now, been somewhat ordinary. It had even been boring, he occasionally thought (though he knew it was necessary work, important work; he knew that people could not exist without dreams). He had worked in the home of a famous actor once, and another time he had followed a circus as it traveled, assigned to give dreams (imagine this!) to a clown.

He had bestowed colorful dreams upon drab, dull people, and he had given grim, colorless dreams to people whose lives were vibrant and exciting. There seemed no real logic or order to the kinds of people and the kinds of dreams they received. It was all in the gathering; it was all dependent on the memories and the fragments and how they fit together in the jigsaw-puzzle world of dreaming. Strapping paid little attention to any of it. He did his job. He did it energetically and according to the rules, but he did it without enthusiasm or interest.

Then he had been assigned to the young woman. The assignment had been a mild punishment for his disinterest. His Heap's leader had simply grown tired of Strapping's casual attitude. She had decided to place him where meticulous attention was badly needed.

Strapping was an orderly sort of fellow, the kind who kept track of things, liked labels and lists and appreciated cleanliness. In his own Heap he was sometimes referred to as a nitpicker because he insisted on designated sleeping places, whereas some other dream-givers preferred to doze simply wherever they flopped down at the end of a busy night.

At first, because of his basic nature, he had been extraordinarily exasperated by the slovenly apartment to which he'd been assigned, and by the sleeping woman who, when he encountered her for the first time, was curled on the couch wearing pajamas with top and bottom unmatched—how irritating that was, to Strapping! He had sighed with despair that first night, looking around, realizing that he was faced with gathering his dream fragments from chipped china, coffee-ringed tables, dirty carpets studded with crumbs, and clothing that had lain unwashed on the floor for days.

But he was a caring fellow. It hadn't taken long before he had realized, through the collected fragments, how sad and needy this young woman's life was, and—because he was keenly intelligent, as well—how great the possibility was that he could help her.

(This was what Dowager had hoped when she assigned the punishment, because she knew her Heap well, and perceived what talents Strapping had to offer, if she could give him the opportunity. It was part of the Old Ones' tasks, to find the right dream-giver for each job. It was why Most Ancient had assigned Fastidious to instruct Littlest One at first, and why, after the transfer of instructors, he was keeping a sharp eye on Fastidious to see if it was time to retire her altogether.)

Now Strapping was doing what Dowager had hoped he would do, becoming what she had wanted him to become. He looked around the shabby dwelling place attentively each night, assessing the changes in the young woman's life. He saw her attempts to create a little order. He saw how she had arranged the toys in the second, unoccupied bedroom, lining up the Matchbox cars on a shelf, placing the baseball cap on the bedpost after she had picked it up from the floor, where it had lain untouched for days.

He noticed that she had bought, though not opened, a package of nicotine patches, and that she had begun to smoke on the back porch and had opened the windows to air the place, and he could smell the difference.

The mail was no longer stacked unopened on the kitchen table beside the dirty coffee cups. The cups were washed and put away, and now the envelopes were in the wastebasket, and the opened bills lay on the table beside her small calculator and her checkbook.

He found himself beginning to hope for her future and to care for her in a way he had not before cared. As she slept restlessly on the couch with the TV a late-night blur across the room, he chose carefully what to touch and gather: the broken seashell once again, the little baseball cap, the bronzed baby shoes that she used for bookends. He wanted to give her dreams of a future with her son.

23

"It's almost Labor Day, John. Do you know what that means?" The woman was washing the few breakfast dishes while the little boy measured dog food from a bag into Toby's bowl.

"World Series?" he asked. "Eat it," he added, speaking firmly to the dog, who was sniffing the blue ceramic bowl, "because you're not getting any more of my bacon ever again."

The woman, standing at the sink, laughed. "You should never leave your plate where he can reach it," she reminded him. "He's shameful."

John scowled. "I was going to sit on the floor and read the funnies while I finished eating. How was I supposed to know he was going to be so grabby?"

"That's why they say 'Live and learn,'" she told him.

They both watched while Toby finally leaned toward his bowl and began to eat the dry dog food.

"You know that dog food that comes in cans?" John asked suddenly. "It smells horrible. And it looks like throw-up."

"Well, it probably smells delicious to dogs. But Toby can't eat that kind. It upsets his stomach."

"I know a guy who ate it."

"A human? Goodness." The woman wrinkled her nose. She hung up the dishtowel and sat down at the table where her mug of tea was waiting. "Why would a person do that?"

"It was a kid. He was just little."

"Oh. Poor little thing. He didn't realize it was dog food, I suppose. Parents have to be so careful. They have to keep a close eye on very little ones. I saw in a catalogue that there is a special latch that you can put on the cupboard under the sink. You know where I keep the cleaning things?" She pointed. "If a toddler got into that cupboard, he might try to take a nibble of Comet, or a sip of ammonia!"

"That's dumb. It would taste terrible."

She chuckled. "But you said you knew of a little one who tasted dog food! I wouldn't think that would be so delicious!"

John didn't laugh. "His father made him do it," he said.

"His father? I don't understand."

"He was bad."

103

"Who was bad, the father?"

"No, the boy, stupid!" John glared at her.

"But—?"

"He was running around the house naked, see. He was just out of the bathtub. He was only little. Three, maybe."

The woman smiled. "That doesn't sound bad. It sounds very sweet."

"Shut up!"

"John," she said to him, "what's wrong?"

"He was running around with no clothes on and he peed on the floor! Like a dog! Like a stupid dog! It was bad! And so the father rubbed his face in it, because that's what you do with dogs!"

"John?"

"I said SHUT UP!"

The boy's face was contorted. "It hurt him. When the father rubbed his face on the floor, it really hurt him. But he didn't cry. He never cries. Cry and you get hit."

The woman nodded, watching him.

"And then the father said that if he was acting like a dog, he had to eat dog food. And that's what they gave him for dinner. That canned stuff. They put it in a bowl on the floor and told him to eat like a dog."

"Who is *they*, John? I thought you were talking about a father."

"Well, there was a mother too, stupid! She put the bowl on the floor. He told her to! The father told her to, and she did!"

The woman nodded. "The poor little boy," she said.

"No, the *dumb* little boy! And bad! It was his own fault! And then he wouldn't eat the dog food."

"Of course he wouldn't."

"So he didn't get anything to eat that night. And in the morning, when it was time for breakfast, think there were Cheerios or anything?"

"No. I think I know what happened."

"He was so stupid he thought there would be Cheerios! But it was the same dog food. And for lunch, same dog food, and for dinner, same dog food, and he was only little, and hungry, and finally he *ate* it! And his father laughed at him!

"'Ha ha ha!'" The little boy imitated harsh laughter. He rocked back and forth in his chair and kicked his legs against it.

"And his mother? I bet his mother didn't laugh, did she?"

His rocking subsided and he leaned forward. "No. She cried, and got hit," he said in a low voice. "She always got hit."

Finished with his breakfast, Toby padded over to the table where the two were sitting. He gazed up at John.

"WHAT ARE *YOU* LOOKING AT, STUPID?" The boy jumped from his chair, overturning it so that it fell against the wall and knocked a small potted geranium from the windowsill onto the floor. Then he ran from the room.

The woman sat silently at the table. She thought about the coming holiday weekend, Labor Day, and what she had planned to tell the boy: that school was about to start.

24

"It's coming back tonight. I can feel it." Littlest shuddered and looked up at Thin Elderly. They had just slid in under the door.

Thin Elderly stood poised, listening and feeling. "Yes," he told her. "The air is tainted. They're on the way."

"They?" Littlest asked in a worried voice.

"Yes. More than one. Shhh." Thin Elderly tilted his head and she could feel that he was holding his breath. After a moment he turned to her. "Smell that?" he asked.

Nervously she sniffed. "Yes," she whispered. "Like garbage, and something burning. Something awful."

He nodded. "We've smelled it before, when we huddled and he inflicted on the boy. But this is worse because they're coming together. It's the

Horde. Everything is multiplied, even the stench."

"Should we hide?" she asked him, wide-eyed.

"No. They don't want us. They're after him." He gestured up the stairs toward the boy's bedroom door.

"But why the Horde this time?" Littlest One was very frightened. The memory of the hot breath, the pawing hooves, the rank odor, and the dreadful hiss was terrifying to her. But it was true that the Sinisteed had not shown any interest in the dream-givers as they huddled together in the hallway. So she was not frightened for herself. It was because of the boy. The Sinisteed had done such damage to him already! She was frightened on his behalf.

"They know we've strengthened him. It's made them angry. That's why they've gathered the Horde," Thin Elderly told her.

"I fear for the woman tonight, as well," he added. "I think they're coming to inflict on both, tonight."

"The dog, too?" Littlest asked in a small voice. She sucked her thumb briefly.

"No. They don't bother with pets. Shhh." He tilted his head and listened again. "They're still some distance away. It seems they're holding back. Waiting. Maybe for the sleep to deepen. That gives us a little time."

"Time for what?"

Thin Elderly sighed. "More strengthening. It's all we can do, really."

He looked at her and she hastily put her hand, with its damp thumb, behind her back. "Do you have any fragments stored?" he asked her.

"A few. Not many. I always like to give him big, complicated dreams, so I use a lot of my fragments. I did one the other night that had the beach, and a kite, and I combined it with food things: ice cream, and something called a hot dog"—she grinned—"and then I added in Toby and Hee-Haw, both, so they all got mixed up in a big convoluted happiness dream.

"Do you like that word, *convoluted*?" she asked shyly. "I just learned it."

"Good for you. You can add words to dreams, you know."

She nodded. "I'm working on it."

Thin Elderly sat on the lowest stairstep. His knee jiggled nervously. He was thinking.

"We don't have time to gather new things," he said finally. "So take what you have left. Are they pretty good fragments?"

She nodded. "A baseball game. He got a hit and felt proud. I have that, still. And a time his mother sang him a funny song."

"Good. Combine those."

"And just yesterday his butterfly was born! It came out of the chrysalis. He's going to let it go tomorrow. But I touched it! The wings were still damp!"

"All right. That's a good one. Add the dog, maybe, and some words. *Laughter* would be a great choice, and *courage*. Bestow as quickly as you can. I'll do the same for the woman. I've saved some good ones from that afghan on the sofa."

"I'll add words to her bestowal as well. *Peace*, I think, for her. And maybe—" He stopped to think. "*Family*."

There was a noise outside, in the distance. A whinny. Littlest One and Thin Elderly held hands and listened.

"We must hurry," Thin Elderly said. "They're preparing to come."

Littlest One fluttered quietly to the stairs and they started up. "When you're done," Thin Elderly whispered, "meet me—"

"In the corner of the hall, where we always huddle?"

He shook his head. "No. We might get trampled there, when the whole Horde comes through."

"Where, then?" She could tell that he was very nervous, and it terrified her. He had always been so calm and reassuring before.

They were in the upstairs hallway now, between the bedrooms. Outside, in the near distance, the noise was increasing. Hoofbeats. Shrill, agitated whinnies.

"The attic," Thin Elderly said. "Meet me in the attic. Now go. *Hurry.* Help the boy!"

They separated and Littlest One fluttered quickly to the place where the boy slept, still unaware of the impending danger.

25

John turned over in the bed without waking. One arm clutched the ragged donkey, and the other was curled around his pillow. He slept with his mouth open, but his breathing was quiet and his sleep was sound.

He heard nothing. He never heard the tiny nightly flutters as Littlest One arranged herself carefully by his ear and sent shimmers of sparkles into his consciousness. Ordinarily it was a quick bestowal, a tiny moment when she sent him a dream, wished him well, and fluttered away. But tonight she had much harder work to do.

She tried to put the Horde sounds out of her consciousness, not to be distracted by the danger or by her own fear. She recited to herself the sequence of directions:

Flutter.

Hover (she was already there, hovering).

Center.

Looking down at the sleeping boy, she centered herself, taking deep breaths, ignoring her own terror, blocking out the horrifying sounds of the fast-approaching enemy. *Breathe,* she thought. *Breathe deeply.* After a moment she felt calm and composed. Then:

Gather! she commanded herself.

From all her resources she sought the fragments she had been holding. She wrenched them forward, reaching far into herself, pulling them from the deepest corners, unfolding things that had been tucked away, arranging them in sequence. She gathered them and held them, and the volume of them almost suffocated her; she felt as if she might explode. But she held on. Then, one by one, she began the bestowals.

The baseball game: the curved line of stitches on the ball and then the high thwacking sound of the hit; the smell of an oiled leather glove; the rough feel of the fabric of a uniform with its dirt-encrusted knees; the thick pad of first base under his hand; the mingled shouts and cheers of the neighborhood crowd.

She leaned forward and with a shimmer of sparkles bestowed it on the boy. Next, the song. She had found it in the boy's treasured photograph of the young woman: a memory of her singing to the boy curled in her lap. A funny song. Littlest couldn't make out the words, really, but she could the melody, and she heard the sound of the boy laughing, and she felt the rhythmic rocking of the chair.

She leaned forward again, and the tiny sparkling bestowal entered the boy. She saw his mouth move slightly into the curved shape of a smile.

She found that she was breathing hard and it was becoming difficult to hover. She had combined fragments before, to create the complicated dreams that she thought he would like. But she had never done more than one bestowal at a time. Now, after two, she was tired, and still, within her, there was so much more to give. And so little time left.

The dog next. The dog was so important! She gathered the feel of silky warm fur under his collar, around his neck, behind his ears, the places that the boy liked to scratch. She added in the cool moistness of the black nose, the thump of the tail against the floor, and the liquid look of his brown eyes as he gazed upward at the boy.

There! She bestowed it in a tiny radiant burst.

But she could feel that she was beginning to falter. Her hover was weak. She breathed deeply again, collecting what strength remained in her. She sorted in her mind through the remaining fragments, in case she had to stop. What was the most important of those she had left?

The butterfly. Of course! She had never bestowed the butterfly on him before, because it was new to him—and to her, too, with its damp, unfolding golden wings. The dried chrysalis was empty now, just papery discarded pieces at the base of the jar. She hadn't bothered to touch them at all. What mattered was the new and vibrant life, resting there on the twig he had carefully placed for it. Remembering the prohibition against the touching of living creatures, Littlest had known she was breaking a rule. But it had seemed so important. She had used her tiniest, most delicate touch, not wanting to frighten or damage the butterfly. But the fragments she had gathered there were very strong, and she could feel them again now as she gathered them closer and closer to her surface: Flying! Beginning! She leaned down and bestowed those feelings upon the boy.

Then, just the tiniest bit of the seashell; she had given it to him often before, so she needed only a reminder of it. And the donkey, silly old Hee-Haw. She was tempted to leave the donkey out, but then it seemed important: the patchedness of it, the lumpy comfort.

She bestowed those, and with them went the last of her energy. She was very shaky now.

But she knew he needed the words. And so she summoned them and breathed them into his ear:

Laughter.

Courage.

But they took everything she had left, and she could not sustain her hover or flutter away. She heard the Horde stampede coming through the wall as she fell. Her strength completely gone, she curled into a ball, into the smallest she could make herself, and rolled under the boy's bed, just out of the way of the stomping, flailing hooves.

∾

The little boy had not heard the pawing at the exterior wall of the house, or the snorting of dilated nostrils as the huge creatures breathed themselves through, sweaty sides heaving and rippled with power. His sleep was undisturbed by the hot *whoooosh* and *hisssss* as they transferred the horrors they carried into his small being.

Across the hall, in the bedroom with pink rosebuds and ribbon garlands on its wallpaper, the woman, too, slept unaware, as did her dog. Thin Elderly had bestowed on her every fragment of contentment he could muster before he fluttered back down, slid, exhausted, under the door to the attic stairs, and made his way up to the place he and Littlest had agreed to meet. Behind him he heard the Horde enter, and he thought he must hug Littlest tightly so that she would not be terrified by such a horrible sound: Hundreds of hooves! The snorting and whinnying! And the smell, too, was awful. Tired though he was, he hurried up the attic stairs to find her and reassure her that they had done all they could.

She was so brave, he thought, for such a tiny thing. So diligent! For all of her playing and dancing and merriment and curiosity, she was a hardworking little dream-giver, devoted to the job. He decided that he would suggest to Most Ancient, when they returned, that Littlest One be given a special commendation for tonight's work. No other dream-giver for decades had had to face a Horde, and none as small as Littlest had *ever* done so. She should be honored in some special way.

Pleased with his idea (but he wouldn't mention it to her, he decided; it would be a surprise; he could picture her look of surprise and her delighted laughter), he reached the top of the stairs and called into the attic, hoping she could hear him above the terrible Horde sounds below.

117

"Littlest?"

But the attic was empty. Frantically, Thin Elderly searched. When he realized that she had not made it, that she had been trampled and scorched by the creatures below, that she had been crushed and kicked aside as they went about their evil work, Thin Elderly huddled, grief-stricken, in the corner of the attic. Head in his arms, he wept.

26

The little boy was someplace strange: a field of some sort, and he was wearing a cap. Yes: a baseball field, that's what it was. There was a scoreboard that said 00, and he held a bat and squinted from under his cap, hoping to hit the pitched ball that came toward him. There were crowds watching. He hoped they would cheer.

But he fell. Someone had pushed him from behind, and now his face was in the dirt. When he tried to get up, the person behind him held him there so he became paralyzed; he couldn't move at all, and the man rubbed his face in the dirt. Hard. There were pebbles in the dirt, sharp bits of rocks, and his face was bleeding, and the man kept laughing and laughing and the boy couldn't understand why, or what he had done to make this happen.

❧

The room was quiet now, for the beasts had gone, their work completed. Silently Littlest One uncurled herself, moved out from under the bed, and stood up on wobbly, tired legs. She could hear the boy moving restlessly and she tried to flutter up, but her fluttering energy had not yet returned. She stood on tiptoes to watch him and could see that his sleep was very troubled. He thrashed in the bed.

There was nothing left, she thought, for her to do to help him, except to hope with all her being. She stood very still, closed her eyes, clenched her tiny teeth, made her hands into little fists, and willed the dreams that she had given him to work their power.

∾

Then, suddenly, a woman began to sing. Her voice was one that had a smile in it, and she sang, "I went to the animal fair, the birds and the beasts were there—" It made him laugh. They both laughed, he and the woman, and he was able to get up now because the man had disappeared.

He reached for the bat, and the crowd cheered because he had overcome something terrible. It was better than a home run, the overcoming! He felt so strong! He turned to show the woman how strong he was, how proud of being strong, but now he could see that the man was there again; now he was hitting the woman—hitting her in the face over and over, saying, "Stupid broad, stupid broad," and when he tried to run and help her he couldn't move. He was very small, suddenly, and naked, and his mouth was full of something that tasted terrible. The man was shoving more and more of it into his mouth and ordering him: "Swallow! Swallow!"

∾

Laughter, Littlest thought, with all her being, as she stood resolutely on the braided rug beside the boy's bed. *Courage!*

∾

"The big baboon, by the light of the moon, was combing his auburn hair . . ." The woman had begun to sing again. How strong she was, he thought! She had escaped the man! And the song was funny! He began to laugh, and when he did, the thick dog food fell from his mouth to the ground, and there was Toby, scarfing it down! How funny that was! The woman saw that and laughed with him, and the man was angry, but the laughter took his power away altogether. He was useless now, the man. He disappeared. The man was gone, and the woman sang, and they laughed and laughed, and *then the boy picked up the bat and hit the ball and the crowd cheered and cheered and cheered, and beside him, as he ran the bases, fluttering there just by his shoulder, was a yellow butterfly—*

∾

Littlest opened her eyes and looked. The boy was smiling now in his sleep. *I did it!* she thought with joy, and hoped that Thin Elderly would be proud of her.

Thin Elderly! Where was he? She wanted to tell him about the boy. She wanted to hear about the woman, to know whether their hard work had been able to save the pair. Littlest rushed to the hall and looked around, but he was not in sight. Suddenly, just as she was beginning to panic, she remembered their agreement to meet in the attic. They had been so rushed, so scared, with the Horde approaching, that they had made the plan in a hurried way, and she had almost forgotten. How worried he would be! She scampered down the hall, her energy beginning to return now, slid under the door, and ran up the dusty staircase, calling his name. He came to her from the corner where he had been huddled, wiping tears from his face, and took her into his arms.

"I thought I'd lost you," he told her.

"I'm safe! I hid!" Littlest said. "And the boy is all right! I watched while he had a nightmare, but then the dream pieces came to him and he smiled and the nightmare went away!"

Thin Elderly smiled in relief. "Littlest," he said, "we do such important work. Sometimes we forget that. Let's go down now and check on the woman."

Together they descended the attic stairs, tiptoed to the door of the pink flowered bedroom, and peered inside. On his bed, the dog, Toby, snored lightly and moved his legs as if he were running in his sleep.

"I gave him a very quick fragment of squirrel-in-park, just to keep him occupied," Thin Elderly explained in a low voice.

A moan sounded from the bed. "Oh, dear," said Littlest, hearing it.

They both watched as the woman tossed her head and whimpered. "She's caught in a nightmare," Thin Elderly murmured in distress.

∿

She stood helplessly, watching as a tiny child crouched on the floor. "Eat it!" a man was saying, and pushing the little boy's face into a bowl. In the background, a woman wept, and she was weeping, too, but both of them were powerless. "Eat it! Eat it!" the man kept snarling, but the child refused. He looked up at her and she reached toward him—

✺

"Hold my hand," Littlest whispered. "Hope with all your heart. And think the words." She reached over and took Thin Elderly's hand and together they wished dream strength into the woman. *Peace*, they thought. *Family.*

✺

—and suddenly it was not that child at all, but her own self, her own little-girl self, wrapped in a soft blanket, with a woman, a mother, reading her a story, and outside it was snowing.

But where was the tortured boy? She looked around, out into the snow, thinking he would be cold, but he was not there—he was here with her, wrapped beside her in the blanket!

Then someone began to cry. Several people were crying. One was a young soldier, who leaned toward her, but he was pulled away, and there was a sound of shots, and she could hear him weeping, but only for an instant, because she looked down then and the little boy was there, smiling, and he was the soldier, or perhaps the son of the soldier, or the memory of the soldier. He was alive, and happy, and he held a stuffed donkey, and a dog was there, too. The boy and the dog and the donkey were her family, and no one was crying anymore, and the snarling man had gone away, and they were all together and safe. It was peaceful.

∾

Her breathing slowed and became soft and regular. She smiled. Whatever had troubled her had ended. Thin Elderly and Littlest One relaxed. "She's fine," Thin Elderly said. "She's going to be fine."

"We did it!" Littlest said proudly.

"Well," Thin Elderly replied, "we helped."

He took her hand. "It's almost morning," he pointed out. "We must hurry back. The others will already be back in the Heap."

"Well, they didn't have to deal with the Horde," Littlest pointed out importantly, "the way we did."

Downstairs, they slid under the door and out into the last of the night.

Littlest looked around as they began their journey back. "Where is the Horde now?" she asked.

"Out there," Thin Elderly told her. "They are always out there."

27

Meticulously the young woman typed her son's name and created a place for him in Mrs. MacMahon's third grade class. He was a document now. He had a permanent place in her computer. John was part of a large group, since all of the Rosewood Elementary students were there, listed alphabetically and then individually, with their grades and their food allergies and their emergency numbers and their authorized pick-up-from-school people and their medical histories. John's chicken pox was there, and his ear infections, and the name of his doctor, and his broken arm—

She shuddered briefly, remembering last year's fracture; John was seven then. Duane still lived with them, and they lived in fear, she and John: what kind of mood would he be in when he came home (if he came home)? Sometimes he was Fun Daddy, laughing and as boisterous as a boy. But more and more by then, by the time John was seven, Duane was someone else, the person he had turned into, the person they didn't know, the person they feared.

They thought it was their fault. If they were nicer, or if she cooked better, or spent less money, or picked up the toys, or if they kept their hair combed a different way, then Fun Daddy would come back. So they tried. And sometimes it worked; that was what always threw her off balance, that it worked sometimes, and she could wheedle him out of his ugly mood and it would be the three of them again, laughing. But this happened less and less often. And not that night, the night he broke John's arm, the night she called the cops, the night she said "no more."

"Coming for coffee?" The school nurse leaned through the door and pointed to her watch. Break time.

She smiled and nodded. "Just typing in my boy's records. He's starting third grade. Look!" She pointed proudly to the computer screen, to the name "JOHN."

The woman came closer and bent down to look. "I didn't know you had a son. Is this his picture?" She picked up a small framed photograph from the desk and smiled at the little boy in a baseball uniform.

"Yes. He's eight."

"Was he here last year?"

She shook her head. "No. We moved over the summer."

"He your only one?"

She nodded.

"Hard," the nurse said, "with you working. What's he been doing all summer? Camp?"

"No. He's been visiting someone." She darkened the computer screen and they started down the hall toward the teachers' lounge where they all had coffee together on the midmorning break.

"A grandma? My kids go to their grandmother's."

"John doesn't have a real grandmother. They're both dead. But this woman's like a grandmother—a fake one, I guess . . ."

"A surrogate grandmother," the nurse said, smiling. "Lucky kid."

"Yes. And he's going to keep staying with her for a while. She'll bring him to school each day."

The guidance counselor held the door to the teachers' lounge open for them.

"I still have to get my act together. I had a whole lot of problems. I've had sort of a tough time since I got divorced."

The guidance counselor, overhearing the comment, said with a grin, "Haven't we all!"

128

Tears, suddenly, came to the young woman's eyes. Embarrassed, she brought her hand to her face, but it didn't help; she couldn't hold the tears back. "Oh!" she said. "I'm sorry!"

The fifth grade teacher, looking up from the table where he was going through a stack of papers, noticed her, stood, and came forward. "What's wrong?" he asked.

Stupid broad. Crying.

She cringed. Apologized. Hid her face.

One by one, though, they hugged her.

John's mother took a deep breath and wiped her eyes. "Sorry!" she said. "I don't know what came over me!" She tucked a loose strand of hair behind her ear and reached for the coffee mug that had her name magic-markered onto it. Each time she entered this room, she felt as if she had found a home.

∾

"And my mom will be there? You're sure?"

"Right there in the office, at her desk. We'll stop in to see her before we go to the classroom. Remember the office where I took you to visit last week?"

He nodded and adjusted the belt that held up his

jeans. "You think my mom is pretty?" he asked.

"I do."

"She's like a movie star."

"Yes, I could see how beautiful she is. And I could see how much she loves you."

"My dad really loves her a lot. The only reason he went to California was because he got a really good job there. He's like a millionaire almost. He's going to buy us a really good car, not junky like yours. He's maybe buying a Ferrari."

"That would be exciting. Is everything stowed in your backpack?"

He nodded. "Yeah. Where's my jacket?"

"Right here." She handed it to him. "What's this in the pocket?"

"My lucky shell."

He showed her, and the woman turned it over in her hands. She recognized the small pink seashell that had been on the table beside his bed. It curved into itself, with a deep coral color at its center. "It's so lovely," she said.

"Yeah. Me and my mom were at the beach. We picked up shells. She kept one but hers was kind of broken. This one was the best. This is my favorite. It's a lucky one."

"It's very fragile, John. Breakable. You've done a great job of taking care of it so far. But I'd hate for it to get broken. Do you think it's a good idea, taking it to school?" She gave it back to him.

"I need it for luck."

She nodded. "Would you trust me to take care of it during the day? I could keep it safe for you here. You know you'll be coming back here to sleep for a while, until your mom is ready for you."

He stroked the little shell. "You think other kids might break it, at school?"

"Not purposely. But it's so delicate, John, that even if someone bumped into you in the hall, it could shatter."

"I wouldn't care. I'd punch anyone who bumps into me."

For a moment he made an angry face. He threw a feigned punch. "I'd get a gun. I'd—"

He looked at her. "I don't want to leave it behind. I need it."

"I have an idea, then. We'll let your mom take care of it each day. How about that? She can keep it on her desk. I noticed that she didn't have any decorations except for that little framed photograph of you. Your seashell could stay right beside that picture."

His face brightened. "Then we'd both have good luck!"

"You certainly would."

He zipped his jacket, with the shell in his pocket.

She helped him arrange his backpack with its blue straps over his thin shoulders.

At the door he turned. The dog, lying on the kitchen floor, drummed his tail on the pine boards. "Toby," John said, "you can't come. But I'll be back here after school. I'll give you a biscuit when I get home."

Walking to the car, he said to the woman with a swagger, "Toby likes me better'n you." She laughed at his boast. John looked up at her and grinned.

28

Littlest One and Thin Elderly were returning to the Heap in the earliest dawn. It was fall. She walked beside him happily, fluttering away occasionally to pick a late flower or gather a dry, brightly colored leaf. She was proudly wearing the golden badge that she'd been awarded by Most Ancient, the badge that honored her courage.

❧

Tonight had been an ordinary night, a night with no battles to fight, and it was a quiet, companionable trip back, the two of them side by side.

"I'm so glad the boy is fine," Littlest said. "I gave him a fun going-back-to-school dream now that he's getting used to third grade. He has some school-books now that I touched. Spelling and such."

"The woman is fine, too," Thin Elderly replied. "Less lonely. Busier. And very, very proud of the boy.

"You were good with the boy, Littlest," he added. "I hope your next assignment is a house with a child in it."

"My next assignment?" she asked, startled.

"Yes, now that you don't need to work with an instructor. Now that you've learned what you needed to know, and grown up—"

"Oh, I haven't, Thin Elderly! I haven't grown up at all! I still play and act foolish! Look!" she said. She threw herself forward in a cartwheel, then a somersault, and turned pleadingly toward him.

He laughed slightly, watching her. "Your playfulness serves you well. It served the boy well. But it's time—"

"You mean my job is ending? Oh, *please* don't say my job is ending!" Suddenly she was bewildered and near tears.

Thin Elderly, weary, was plodding along. He yawned. "Of course not. People always need dreams. Their whole lives, they must dream.

"The boy will be leaving that house eventually, though. And you will be, too. You'll be reassigned, now that you've proven yourself.

"Hurry, dear," he reminded her. "It's getting early." He looked toward the east, where the sky was lightening.

"Oh," Littlest said in relief, "you mean I'll go to his new house! I do hope it will have lots of things to touch! I was a little worried," she confided, "because he had so *few* things in the woman's house. But it turned out all right, didn't it?" She twirled around happily and leaned down to pick another wildflower.

"No, you'll probably have a completely new assignment. Another dream-giver already has the house that the boy will be moving to, the place where his mother lives."

Littlest stopped twirling. She looked at Thin Elderly in despair. "But—" She began to speak, then stopped herself. She looked embarrassed. Finally she moved close to Thin Elderly and spoke in an extremely small and private voice, directly into his ear.

"I love the boy," she whispered.

He looked shocked. He spoke firmly to her. "You mustn't. You can't. It isn't permitted."

She touched his hand and reminded him of something. "But remember that time when you thought the Horde had gotten me?"

He nodded.

"You cried," she pointed out. "I could tell you'd been crying! And didn't that mean . . .?"

Thin Elderly recalled that terrible time. He sighed. "It was a lapse," he explained. "I am not a perfect dream-giver. I let myself, just for a moment, feel something that we are not allowed to feel."

"Why not?" she asked him.

"Love is a human emotion. And we are not human."

There it was. He said it with such certainty. And it was the thing she had always wondered, the thing she had asked about again and again. No one had ever given her a true answer. Now she felt—she *knew*—that Thin Elderly was telling her the truth. So. She was not human.

"What am I, then? What are we?" she asked.

He took a deep breath. This was always so hard to explain. "We are imaginary," he told her gently, "and we live within."

She frowned. "We live in the Heap," she pointed out.

He nodded. "The Heap is within."

"Within *what?*"

"Within the stories. Within the night. Within the dreams," he explained.

She thought for a long time. Then she used her tiniest voice again. "Am I within the boy?" she whispered.

"Always," he said, and smiled at her.

It made sense to her, and she asked nothing else. Littlest sighed and fluttered ahead and around him, playing in the last of the night that remained, using her youthful energy.

"Look!" she called to him, and pointed to her own shadow, then danced a bit, waving her arms to make the shadow dance and wave as well. "It's a phenomenon of light!"

He chuckled, watching her, but reminded her again, "We must hurry. We mustn't be out and about when the sun rises."

"All right." She fluttered back near him, then stopped, suddenly, examining her own self. "My goodness!" she exclaimed. "I'm not transparent anymore!" She peered at her own arm, then lifted a leg and looked carefully at that as well. "I can't see through me!

"Can you?" she asked him, and thrust her arm into his face. "Can you see through me?"

"No. You're becoming somewhat solid. You're filling in," he explained.

"What fills me?" she asked, staring still at her arm.

"Everything that you're a part of. Your own story fills you."

"What happens to me now?" she asked in a worried voice. "I've never been solid before."

"You're not solid *yet*. You're *becoming* solid. I'd call you translucent, I think, at this stage. Look. Hold your arm next to mine."

She did so, and they could both see the difference. His arm was opaque, quite firm, and hers still glimmered with backlight. But it was true that she was no longer transparent.

"What happens now?" he said, repeating her question. "You bring all of that solidity to your work. And someday perhaps you will use it to teach a young dream-giver."

They hurried on but her brow was furrowed. She tugged at his arm, stopped him, and looked up into his wise, kind eyes.

"I feel terribly sad," Littlest One confided, "about the boy, and about the filling-in."

"Quite so. Change means leaving things behind, and that's always sad. Please hurry now. There's the Heap just ahead, and look: the sun is about to rise. Dive in."

Together they dove into the Heap just as the sky turned pink behind them.

"Cutting it a little close," Most Ancient scolded.

He had been standing at the entrance, watching for them.

"Yes. I'm sorry. Littlest just noticed that she's beginning to turn solid, and we stopped to talk about it."

Most Ancient sighed. "Ah. Change. But we all go through it. Go on and rest, Thin Elderly. You look exhausted."

Thin Elderly yawned and moved into the darkness. Most Ancient turned to Littlest.

"Are you all right?" he asked. "I have a surprise for you."

Littlest One was still examining her own self, holding her different parts toward the entrance where the dawn light now glowed. Ahead, in the Heap, where the other dream-givers were already nestled to sleep, and where Thin Elderly had gone to join them, it was dark. "Yes," she said, a little uncertainly, "I'm fine. Just adjusting."

Then, recalling what he had said, she turned to him eagerly. "What's my surprise?"

Most Ancient turned and reached for something that was behind him. He picked it up and placed it in her arms, and it looked up at her with wide, curious eyes. It was what she had once been: tiny, a wisp of a thing, with a mischievous smile and a trusting, visible heart.

"Oh!" she cried. She hugged it to her, against her badge. "What's its name?"

"Ask it," Most Ancient suggested.

"Who are you?" she asked the diminutive, transparent creature in her arms, keeping her voice calm and quiet so that it wouldn't be scared.

"New Littlest," it told her.

She was puzzled and almost frightened at first. Then she thought, *Of course!* Most Ancient could not always have been Most Ancient, and Thin Elderly must once have been something else. Even Fastidious—well, maybe not. Perhaps she had always been Fastidious.

She cradled New Littlest, moving her hands as gently as possible around the fragile little thing, and turned back to ask Most Ancient what she needed to know.

"Who am I now?"

"Gossamer," he told her.